P9-CMX-848

A TALE OF TWO PRETTIES

A TALE OF TWO PRETTIES

A CLIQUE NOVEL BY
LISI HARRISON

poppy

LITTLE, BROWN AND COMPANY
New York   Boston

CLIQUE novels by Lisi Harrison:

THE CLIQUE

BEST FRIENDS FOR NEVER

REVENGE OF THE WANNABES

INVASION OF THE BOY SNATCHERS

THE PRETTY COMMITTEE STRIKES BACK

DIAL L FOR LOSER

IT'S NOT EASY BEING MEAN

SEALED WITH A DISS

BRATFEST AT TIFFANY'S

THE CLIQUE SUMMER COLLECTION

P.S. I LOATHE YOU

BOYS R US

CHARMED AND DANGEROUS: THE RISE OF
THE PRETTY COMMITTEE

THE CLIQUETIONARY

THESE BOOTS ARE MADE FOR STALKING

MY LITTLE PHONY

A TALE OF TWO PRETTIES

ALPHAS novels by Lisi Harrison:

ALPHAS

MOVERS AND FAKERS

BELLE OF THE BRAWL

Copyright © 2011 by Alloy Entertainment

All rights reserved. Except as permitted under the U.S. Copyright Act of 1976, no part of this publication may be reproduced, distributed, or transmitted in any form or by any means, or stored in a database or retrieval system, without the prior written permission of the publisher.

Poppy

Little, Brown and Company
Hachette Book Group
237 Park Avenue, New York, NY 10017
For more of your favorite series, go to www.pickapoppy.com

First Edition: February 2011

Poppy is an imprint of Little, Brown and Company.
The Poppy name and logo are trademarks of Hachette Book Group, Inc.

The publisher is not responsible for websites (or their content) that are not owned by the publisher.

The characters and events in this book are fictitious. Any similarity to real persons, living or dead, is coincidental and not intended by the author.

CLIQUE® is a registered trademark of Alloy Media, LLC.

Cover photos by Roger Moenks
Author photo by Gillian Crane

alloy**entertainment**

Produced by Alloy Entertainment
151 West 26th Street, New York, NY 10001

ISBN: 978-0-316-08442-0

10 9 8 7 6 5 4 3 2 1
CWO
Printed in the United States of America

A LETTER FROM LISI

It is November 29, 2010. I am staring at my computer screen, faced with one of the biggest challenges of my writing career—and believe me, there have been many. But this one feels more insurmountable than all of them combined, times ten. Because my editor just asked who I would like to dedicate this final Clique book to. And I seriously can't decide.

My parents for teaching me to love and nurture my inner freak? Yes. My brother and sister for the lifetime of laughter? Yes. My husband for keeping me calm when I am spinning like Johnny Weir without the skates? Yes! The little creatures in my house who kiss me every morning before I go off to work? Mmwah! My ah-mazing editors for their brilliant guidance, contributions, and schedule-juggling? Yes! Yes! Yes! The publicity and marketing teams who remind you that I exist? Absolutely. My publisher and producer for backing me? Indeed. The team at Warner Premiere for turning the Clique into a movie? Certainly. The cast and crew who brought it to life? Uh-huh. My kick-butt agent for being so much more than a kick-butt agent? Given. My attorney and his team for making me feel like family instead of a client? Yup! My friends at MTV for the most inspiring and hilarious years of my life? Of course. Brilliant novelists who fill me with awe? Sure. My BFFs, who have watched me, year after year, vanish into the "cone of silence" while I work on another book; who have heard me say, "This is the last time I will fall of the face of the earth, I promise"—only to watch me disappear again? Definitely. Spell-check for making it seem like I was listening in English class instead of daydreaming? Yesiree. The teachers, librarians, booksellers, bloggers, magazines, newspapers, and critics who have supported this series? You bet-cha. The parents and grandparents who have bought my books and encouraged their kids to read? One hundred percent. The chai tea latte–makers, gum-sellers, food delivery guys, sushi chefs, musicians, scented-candle manufacturers, and Internet inventors who have made it possible for me to stay in my office chair for nine hours a day? Roger that.

Clearly, hundreds are final-dedication contenders. But only one can be worthy. So what does that mean? Is it a sign? Is the universe telling me it's not time to end the Clique? Should I keep writing about the Pretty Committee until I have managed to thank everyone who needs to be thanked? I'll admit, I've considered it. But once again, as sad as it is, I have to stand by my decision and leave while the party is still going.

I know you are disappointed. I have read your letters (thousands) and the comments on my Blah-g (thousands and thousands). But it's time.

In 2002, when I began the Clique, pop culture was different. Materialism was trendy. The more designer initials on a handbag the better. "Who are you wearing?" was more important than what you were wearing. Green stood for money, not the environment. It was a time of excess, and everyone was proud to wear their wealth on their silk sleeves. Friends were upgraded like cell phones and girls seemed more loyal to a lip-gloss brand than their besties.

When I started writing *The Clique*, I wanted to show you how despicable bullying, snobbery, and elitism are by creating a character—Massie Block—who worked tirelessly, and often heartlessly, to maintain her alpha status. My goal was to show you that the so-called perfect girl is far from perfect. And that, more times than not, she's more insecure than the no-so-perfect girls—Claire Lyons and Layne Abeley. You got it *wayyyy* before the grownups did. I knew you would.

Now, eight years later, things are very different. The economy has tanked. Snatching up a killer pair of boots from Target or H&M has become a bigger source of pride than a $5,000 handbag. National security is the new insecurity. And I pray that the fatal reports of bullying (cyber and live) have forced you all to take an honest look at how you treat others.

I don't feel as compelled to shine a light on shallow behavior as I did in 2002, simply because there is less of it. Is it gone? Sadly, no. But it's not as ubiquitous as it used to be. I also think Massie and the Pretty Committee have learned a lot about themselves and the true meaning of friendship. Are they perfect? Puh-lease. Who is? But they are more grounded than they were when the series began. So am I. Are you?

As long as I write, I will always fill my books with goofiness. That's one thing that will never change. Because that's who I am. And I can't thank you enough for accepting me; for coming back month after month; for joining the biggest Clique in the world; for being final-book dedication worthy.

And so, *A Tale of Two Pretties* is for _____.*
My loyal, brilliant, always improving, wonderfully
imperfect reader. You were, are, and always will be the
wind beneath my freak flag. Until we meet again . . .

I ah-dore you!

Lisi
Harrison

* Insert your name in BIG, BOLD letters.

The frigid night air smelled like fireplaces, pine, and anticipation.

"Just one more second," Cam called from inside his garage.

Claire stomped her candy cane–inspired red-and-white Keds against the asphalt driveway to stay warm. But her chattering teeth had nothing to do with the winter weather and everything to do with excitement.

"And keep your eyes closed!"

She shut them so hard her lids shar-pei'ed, showing Cam that he was a go-the-extra-mile kind of guy and (if she was being Christmas Eve honest) because she was a wee bit nervous. He'd given her gifts before: gummies, burned CDs, framed photos . . . but never anything that required closed eyes and a garage.

Suddenly, the door lifted with a creaky groan. "Okay. Open!"

Either Rudolph's nose had hanged itself or Cam had replaced the regular garage light with a red bulb. At first the dim glow made it hard to see, but once her eyes adjusted, Claire giggled nervously. "What is this?"

"What does it look like?" Cam asked from behind a

microphone, an electric guitar strapped across his green henley. He looked like Justin Bieber minus the cotton swab hairdo.

Harris, his older brother, sat at a rickety drum set behind him, while Massie's ex, Derrington, stood off to the left, with a bass. But the biggest shock was Layne Abeley, who wore a plaid fedora, a long black blazer, black baggy slacks, a white skinny tie, and a saxophone.

"Introducing Garage Band," Cam said.

Claire applauded. The musicians bowed.

"FYI," Layne said into her microphone, "I'm not only the backup vocalist, I'm also the wind section."

"Ha!" Derrington smiled. "She said wind section. *Prrrrrrerpt.*"

Harris laughed at the fart impression.

"Ready?" Cam called. "Introducing, *Gummy Claire.*" Garage Band lifted their instruments. "Five, six, seven, eight."

Harris began drumming a four count, Derrington plucked his bass, and Layne clamped down on the reed mouthpiece and blew. They sounded a like a rock version of "Twinkle Twinkle Little Star." Cam leaned toward the mic and Claire's insides squinched. *What if he was bad? What if he was good? What if she blushed? Was she supposed to dance? Sway? Clap? Cry? Throw her bra onstage? Because she didn't have a bra, just a tank top, and she wasn't about to take it off and—*

Her crush began to sing.

This Christmas I know for sure,
I've got a fever and you're the cure.

This isn't Florida, it's the cold W-C,
But I'll keep you warm my little gummy . . .

Was this really happening? Claire felt so awkward and special at the same time she didn't know where to look. Cam's blue eye? His green one? Or Layne's wind-filled cheeks? She dug deep into the pocket of her blue puffy coat and pulled out a sour reindeer, the limited-edition seasonal special at Sweetsations Candy Shoppe.

Gummy, Gummy, Gummy Claire,
Everything sucks when you're not there,
You inspired me to write this ditty,
And even won over the Pretty Committee . . .

Cam said he wanted to exchange Christmas gifts, but she hadn't expected this Jo Bros–like serenade. A jolt of affection—or was it the limited-edition sugar rush?—made Claire's crush levels soar higher than a reindeer in a rocket.

I stand before you with my guitar,
Cause I'm not old enough to drive a car,
When I am, ride shotgun with me,
Off into a sunset of sweet candy.
Gummy, Gummy, Gummy Claire,
Everything sucks when you're not there.

The song ended with a soulful wail from Layne, and the Garage Band bowed.

Claire let go of the breath she hadn't realized she'd been holding, and then broke into wild applause. Forget the Gondola Wheel at Rye Playland: The Fisher garage, with its shelves stocked with tools, bike helmets, and old video games, its cracked cement floor, oil stain patches, and single red bulb, was officially the most romantic place on Earth.

"Merry Christmas," Cam said sheepishly.

"Merry Christmas." She smiled, wishing everyone would stop staring, wondering what she should do next. Because she had zero-minus-a-thousand ideas. "That was awesome, you guys," was all she could manage under such extreme pressure.

"I still think Sax Appeal is a better name," Layne harrumphed, laying her instrument in its foamy case.

"I like Who Cracked Wind," Derrington joked, wiggling and fanning his booty.

When everyone stopped laughing, Harris tossed his drumstick in the air. "Okay, it's Wii time."

"You got Call of Duty: Black Ops?" Layne asked.

"Yup."

"Pearl Harbor Trilogy—1941: Red Sun Rising?"

"Yup," Harris said.

"Shadow of the Ninja?"

He glanced at Derrington in a where-did-you-find-this-girl sort of way and then nodded yes.

"Layne likes," she said, loosening her tie. "Let's do this."

Harris led them into the house, leaving Claire and Cam alone. They had been alone zillions of times but never post-serenade. Suddenly neither one of them knew where to look. So they giggled.

"Wanna sit?" Cam finally asked. He gestured to a worn blue trunk in the far corner by the lawnmower.

Claire lifted the measly present she got Cam and joined him. Why didn't she think bigger? He had filled her heart; she'd filled an elf-covered gift bag.

"I really loved that," she said, kissing him on his Drakkar Noir–scented cheek.

"It was fun," he said modestly. Exhaling a puff of breath into the cold garage he asked, "Do you want to open your gift?"

"You mean there's another one?!" Claire asked, the needle on her Guilt-O-Meter exploding to bits.

Cam reached behind the trunk and presented her with the same elf gift bag.

Awk-ward!

She showed him hers and they laughed like their old selves again. "Wanna open them at the same time?"

He nodded. "On three," he said. "One, two . . ."

"Three!" Claire called, digging in.

Cam did the same. "Uh-oh."

"I know," Claire began. "It's not even close to what you got me. I wish I—"

He was smiling mischievously. "Just open your present."

Claire pushed aside the tissue and gasped. He had given her an old-fashioned candy dispenser filled with red and green M&Ms. Only instead of M&M, the candies read C&C, for

Claire and Cam. Her gift to him was nearly identical. Only she had a picture of them printed on the candies—the one Massie had taken over Thanksgiving weekend.

After a thank-you lip-kiss, they both cracked up again.

Fluffy flakes began falling outside the garage. The quiet street was snow-globe beautiful. Claire's teeth began chattering. If the moment had been any more romantic they would have taken down the tree and called it Valentine's Day.

"There's one more thing in the bag," he said.

"Cam!" Claire's cheeks burned with single-gift guilt.

"Don't worry; it's something for both of us." He twirled a loose thread from his shirt around his finger, then yanked.

Claire pulled a glossy card from the tissue. "'Photography lessons for two'?"

He nodded. "Every Friday for the next ten weeks."

"Cam! It must have cost—"

He lifted his palm to silence her. "It was free. My dad got it for my mom's birthday but she has Current Events Club on Fridays so . . ."

"This is the best!" Claire didn't know what she loved more: the chance to learn about shadows and light and aperture and transparency or the guaranteed date she'd have with Cam every Friday night! Her insides began soaring all over again and then, as if hit by a missile—*Missile Block!*—they came crashing down.

"What?" asked Cam, picking up the trouble signal. And then, realizing, he said, "Oh. Oops."

Oops? Oops was "I dialed the wrong number." Not a call to

arms, which is exactly what would happen if Claire ditched out on Friday night sleepovers with the Pretty Committee. She was finally an accepted member of the group. Turning her back on that would mean war, under the best of circumstances. But now? When Massie was reeling from the news of her father's recent financial crisis? When Claire was the only one who knew? Bailing would be a kamikaze mission. But Friday night photography with Cam . . .

The self-help podcast she and Massie had listened to the night before—"Putting the U in Nutshell"—came to mind. After a multiple-choice quiz, Claire had been deemed a "sympathy-stresser": someone who takes on other people's problems as her own. Massie was a "resist-rejoice": change was unimaginable, but once she tried it on, it fit like couture.

In a nutshell, Claire needed to learn to put her own needs before the needs of others (*class with Cam*) and have faith that Massie—after an apocalyptic freak-out—would eventually respect Claire's pursuit of photographic excellence and might even welcome her back when the ten-week course was through.

Or she could play the bad-sushi card every Friday night until April, and hope no one called her bluff. Which, considering the options, was, without a doubt, the smarter choice.

"We're opening presents in five minutes," Kendra called from the kitchen.

Butter-soaked whiffs of basting turkey greeted Massie as she descended the stairs, a warm pug in her arms and last year's Balenciaga scarf draped over her shoulders.

"Don't get too excited," she told Bean's wagging tail. It was just a Thanksgiving novelty candle, meant to fill the house with the smell of home cooking for those incapable of doing it the old-fashioned way. Kendra had lit one last night, too, hoping to minimize the trauma caused by Inez's furlough. But nothing could replace the housekeeper's gourmet cooking, or change the fact that the Blocks had spent Christmas Eve eating General Tso's chicken from a Chinese take-out restaurant, just like their Jewish friends had. Or that on Christmas Day they'd be microwaving the leftovers.

But the worst part? The Block estate was icier than Jake and Vienna's breakup thanks to the high cost of heating a mansion in December. *Who knew?* It wasn't until Kendra had pointed out that cooler temperatures tightened pores that Massie got on board with a capital *Gawd.*

Unfortunately, the explanation hadn't satisfied Kristen the way it had Alicia, Dylan, and Claire when the sporty blonde couldn't stop shivering at last week's sleepover. So Massie had said that Al Gore had called her father, and as a personal favor asked him to turn down the heat. That seemed to warm Kristen's insides. But little else.

Massie stopped in the scantly decorated oversized living room and sighed. "Is my name Freddy Krueger?" she asked the pug.

Bean's ear twitched.

"Then why am I living in a nightmare?"

The Blocks had a tree, but hiring Sven, the Holiday Cheer Coordinator, to give it the Rockefeller treatment was no longer an option. So now the thin pine—which was leaning left from the unevenly distributed weight of its ornaments—took the *rock* out of Rockefeller and left only the *fell*.

Gone were the glitter-dusted floors, the festive playlists, the well-dressed party guests, the candy-cane chandeliers, the ruby-and-emerald window treatments, the gingerbread doghouse, the grazing reindeer, the gold-tipped mistletoe encouraging *Love, Actually* moments from visitors, the illuminated trees, the snow machine, the ice sculptures, the bustling caterers, the cute valet boys dressed as toy soldiers . . . and Massie's will to live.

She swallowed back a tear like it was a cinnamon skinny latte and shuffled in her Tory Burch sheepskin moccasins to claim the spot in front of the fireplace—the room's sole source of heat. A single log burned, giving off weak gasps of warmth, like it, too, had given up. And worst of all—*worst of all!*—there was just one gift under the boughs, sitting alone like Jennifer Aniston at a couples' retreat.

Bean jumped from Massie's arms and ran circles around the tree, because she could. *I know money is tight,* Massie thought, glaring at the single strand of lights that adorned the crooked tree. *But how poor could we possibly be? Unless . . . what if Mom and Dad are doing this to teach me a lesson? What if we aren't poor at all? What if this is a continuation of that snoozer lecture Dad gave me a few months ago, about how it's tacky to buy a third car because so many people are struggling these days. And the importance of saving money . . . or whatever it was that made me yawn so hard my mascara ran.*

EhMaGawd, that's it! This is all an act. They are trying to scare me straight. Phew times a thousand to the power of ten!

Massie peeked behind the brocade couch in search of her real presents as her father limped in.

"Happy Christmas!" William said, clearly still sore from his attempt to climb a ladder in cashmere socks. He'd been trying to hang mistletoe above the front door when he slipped off the top rung and twisted his ankle.

Or had he? Maybe it was all part of the performance. In which case, bravo!

"Merry merry!" Kendra bellowed, her silky white robe fanning out behind her like a superhero cape as she raced to remove William's slippers before he put them on the couch. Red nail polish was smeared on her cuticles.

Massie winced. "Mom, are you a carpenter?"

"No."

"Then why are you working with nails? Did that trainee at Serenity Spa do that to you? I told you to stick with Olga!"

"Massie," William said warningly. "We're all working to cut back."

". . . And cut! That's a wrap. You've made your point." Massie smiled. "Lesson learned. I'll save my money. Now can we *puh-lease* go back to normal." She shivered. "Before my tongue freeze-sticks to the wand in my lip gloss."

"What lesson?" Kendra lifted a steaming mug to her mouth and blew. The floating coffee grounds spread like rats in a tenement house.

"You know exactly what lesson," Massie said, intent on making them confess before this scene caused lasting damage to her psyche. "I get it okay? Just—" Her iPhone pinged. "Hold on."

Landon, her high-school crush, had sent a text.

Landon: Merry Xmas.

A photo of a square box, wrapped in pearly pink paper with an oversized silver bow, filled her screen and melted her heart. Finally, someone who understood the true meaning of Christmas.

Landon's holiday budget had clearly been bigger than hers. The eighty dollars Kendra gave her wouldn't even cover the cost of that box, let alone whatever was inside. And she still had the Pretty Committee gifts to think of. Massie had had to cancel her order for five personalized, monogrammed, butter-leather messenger bags she'd seen Gwyneth wearing as she GOOPed around London. Instead, she'd gone trick-or-treating at the Saks cosmetic counters and stocked up on the free samples. The PC would receive unflattering shades like Digi-Dazzle and the accompanying *let's-pretend-we're-going-to-St.-Barts-this-holiday* beach bags, while Landon would get a homemade gift certificate that entitled him to an afternoon of shopping with Massie as his style consultant.

She was about to write back to Landon when William cleared his throat. "You know the rules, Massie: No texting by the tree."

Massie set down her phone. "My bad, I thought the 'tree' was a coat rack."

William ignored the dig, plastering a smile on his face. "Present time!"

Kendra handed the lone gift under the "tree" to her daughter, and Massie tore it open, anxious for this charade to end.

Inside sparkled a small black diamond that hung from a gleaming white-gold chain that someone like Kristen or Claire would have been satisfied with. Massie searched the box for the matching earrings and bracelet. She found nothing.

"Isn't it the diamond you wanted?" Kendra asked, her smile faltering.

William waited for her answer, an expectant look on his face.

"Yeah, thanks. I love it." Massie held the diamond up to the light and tried to turn her downward-facing mouth into something resembling happiness. Ever since she saw the entire set of black diamond jewelry in the Barneys catalogue, she had envisioned the drop earrings glistening in tandem with her shiny brown hair and the thick bracelet anchoring her tiny wrist. The necklace—the least impressive member of the group—was a Jessica Simpson piece. It didn't thrive being single.

Flashes of Christmas Gifts Past danced across her mind. Just last night she had flipped through her special Moleskine notebook where she detailed all the gifts she received each year: the exclusive Birkin bag from last Christmas, the walk-on role for *Hannah Montana* the year before that, the trips to London and Bermuda, the MacBooks and iPods, and the dozens of Jimmy Choos and Pradas that had peeked out from her stocking year after year. At least five pages would be crammed with gift descriptions each holiday. This year, unless she wrote in really big letters, her holiday haul list would read like a STOP sign.

Massie couldn't deny it any longer. The Blocks were broke. This wasn't a life lesson. It was the thing life lessons were supposed to prepare her for.

If only she had paid attention.

CURRENT STATE OF THE UNION

IN	OUT
White Christmas	Green Christma$
Shopping at Salvation Army	Donating to Salvation Army
Boo Hoo Hoo	Ho Ho Ho

"Mo-om! You promised me you'd get rid of this!" Kristen exclaimed as she unwrapped the tissue paper from an old ornament. It was a raggedy piece of worn green felt that she had painstakingly cut into the shape of a tree and adorned with glitter during her second-grade art class.

"I lied!" Marsha said, patting Kristen near the base of her high blond ponytail.

Every December Marsha unpacked the ornament from the Rubbermaid storage container stuffed with holiday decorations, blew the dust from it, and hung it proudly on the tree. And every year, Kristen made a show of being mortified, but secretly, she was more GLAD than a trash bag when her mother fought to keep it. What they lacked in family, they made up for in Christmas spirit. And like her mother always said, "Corporate America can't put a price on that."

Cinnamon and spice coated the air, courtesy of the hot apple cider brewing on the stove and the cooling gingerbread cookies Kristen had baked. Marsha's Clay Aiken holiday CD played softly from the boom box under the television, which was set to one of those channels that broadcasted nothing but wintry scenes and burning logs in a fireplace. The plastic tree they used every year was proudly perched in the corner, wearing twinkling multicolored lights, silver garland, and dozens of ornaments that spanned the years—Baby's First Xmas, a picture of a toddler-sized Kristen sitting on Santa's knee at the mall, teddy bears, snowflakes, angels, and balls of every size and color. Massie would have taken one look at it and made some sort of joke about it being less coordinated than Layne Abeley's wardrobe, but Kristen didn't care. It carried more memories than an elephant stampede.

Kristen was just fixing her stocking, which had been hanging crookedly from a tack on the wall, when a knock came at the door. She opened it to find Dempsey Solomon, her next-door neighbor. Blushing, she wrapped her Gap Outlet robe more tightly around her and wished him a Merry Christmas.

Dimples firing, he held out a plate of chocolate chip cookies. "My mom made them. They're gluten-free." He rolled his eyes, but smiled. The warm feeling Kristen had had all morning rose into a heat wave. *Did Dempsey feel it, too?*

Marsha appeared at Kristen's side, her big green eyes beaming.

"What a nice surprise! Come on in and join us for some cider?"

"I'd love to, but I'm heading out to Long Island to see my cousins."

"Oh, we're sorry to hear that," Marsha said, putting her hands on Kristen's shoulders. "And by *we*, I mean Kristen," she tease-winked.

"*Mo-om!*" The heat wave turned into two fireballs on her

cheeks that she could've roasted chestnuts over. Kristen couldn't shut the door fast enough.

"Gift time!" Marsha trilled, probably to avoid a *stop-embarrassing-me* fight with her daughter. It worked. Kristen kicked a fallen ornament out of the way and cheered when it touched the opposite wall, pretending it was the winning goal in a championship game, and then snuggled onto the cozy couch.

David Beckham, Kristen's fat gray cat, leaped onto the seat next to her and then curled into her lap, purring contentedly. Seconds later he was asleep. Earlier, she'd stuffed his paw-shaped stocking with catnip toys, which were now strewn all over the apartment. Kristen made a mental note not to give him all his gifts at once next year. He clearly couldn't handle it.

Her mom held out a large square box, a smile blooming on her face. "This one first."

Kristen attacked the gift like she attacked the sale rack at Nordstrom. Maybe it was the new iPod she'd asked for. Or maybe the ultra-lightweight Nikes she wanted that would fit right in her purse. She tore away layers of sparkly silver wrapping paper and filmy tissue paper to reveal . . .

. . . *a soccer ball?*

It looked like every other soccer ball she owned.

"Thanks, Mom!" Kristen managed. After all, it was a perfectly good soccer ball.

"Anything else in there?" Marsha asked, like she already knew.

Kristen double-checked. Sure enough, a letter lay nestled in the tissue paper. Slowly, she unfolded it and scanned the type.

Dear Ms. Gregory,

Congratulations! You've been accepted to the All-Star Soccer Sisters program—the nation's highest-ranked competitive traveling soccer squad for middle- and high-school girls!

This elite organization . . .

"I've been accepted into the Soccer Sisters!" Kristen screamed. Beckham jumped off her lap and bolted down the hall.

"I know!" Marsha screamed back.

They hugged and jumped around the small living room until Mrs. Krandall, the cranky biddy in the apartment below, poked her ceiling with a broom. Kristen fell back on the couch and bicycled her legs in the air. She'd forgotten she'd even applied to be part of the elite, super-intense squad. Most of the Soccer Sisters' players ended up in Division I programs—and some of them had even made it all the way to the Olympics! Her coach at OCD had singled her out after a particularly tough game early in the season and encouraged her to apply. Kristen had been so sure she wouldn't get in that she never bothered to tell anyone that she'd sent the forms in.

Adrenaline pumping, Kristen paced the cramped living room, stretching her hamstrings and calf muscles every few steps. Her mom picked up the letter and read it aloud.

"'This elite organization takes soccer very seriously . . .'"

"Same." Kristen beamed.

"'Success is the result of extreme determination and hard work . . .'"

"Tell me something I don't know." Kristen was never one to back away from a challenge.

"'. . . Practices are held every weekend—no exceptions—from January through June, taking off for the month of July, and then resuming August through November.'"

Kristen paused mid-lunge. "Every weekend?" *For the rest of eighth grade?* How was that even possible?

Marsha waved the letter. "That's what it says."

Kristen fell back onto the couch and grabbed the letter from her mom, holding it close to her chest. Playing with the Soccer Sisters every weekend meant Kristen would have to sacrifice ah-*lawt*. No more Friday night sleepovers with the PC. No more spa days, courtesy of Massie. No more shopping trips to New York City, courtesy of Dylan's mom. No more hanging out with Dempsey . . .

But she would gain a lot, too, and not just in muscle mass. Soccer was her passion, and she'd be spending weekends with girls who'd rather run the field than play it, who'd rather charge a goalie than a gloss. Girls like her.

Kristen sighed loudly. It was nothing against the Pretty Committee. They were her best friends, her family. But the chance to join the Soccer Sisters . . . to be able to do something she loved and something she excelled at . . .

It was a lose-lose situation. Choosing one meant sacrificing the other, even though it shouldn't have to. Any sane person would have assured Kristen she could have both: friends at school and soccer on the weekends. But "any sane person" didn't know Massie Block.

Meaning this was one Christmas miracle Kristen was going to have to keep to herself.

"Homesweethommmmme," Dylan burped as the stretch Hummer stopped in front of the Marvil house.

The driver suppressed a smile.

"We haven't eaten in days," snapped her sister Ryan. "How are you still burping?"

"Like thissssssss," Dylan burped again.

"Gross," hissed her other sister, Jaime, while her mother checked the screen of her BlackBerry. Despite having just spent ten luxurious days in the Caribbean, everyone was on edge.

Dylan examined her arms closely. Definitely pinker than when she had left on the surprise spa vacation. But Dylan was more taken with the *size* of her skin than its color. And now that she had put her limbs to the final test, checking them in Westchester light, it was confirmed. They were definitely lither.

Merri-Lee had flown her daughters to the Caribbean for a ten-day cleanse: no candy, no soda, no all-you-can-eat yogurt-covered pretzels. It had been impossible at first, but once the Marvils got past their caffeine- and carb-withdrawal headaches, they started feeling pretty good. And Dylan had only cheated six times! She victoriously wiggled her shrunken butt in the heated leather seat. She couldn't wait to show the PC how pink, refreshed, and skinny she was.

Merri-Lee locked the doors and then signaled the driver to raise the partition. "Girlies, one little thing before we go inside." She popped open her monogrammed Chanel compact and began reapplying her Guerlain KissKiss lipstick. "I have a Christmas surprise," she said, blotting her lips on the label of her Evian bottle.

Another surprise? What now? Cutting off our water supply? Dylan and her sisters exchanged curious glances.

"You may want to touch up your faces before you see it," she suggested.

Ryan and Jaime dumped out their makeup kits and got busy. But Dylan couldn't be contained. Just before they left, Merri-Lee had Zachary Levi and Katharine McPhee on her talk show to sing "Terrified" and Zachary's smooth voice—*or was it his face? or his dark features? or maybe his smile*—made her flat-ironed red hair curl. All week Dylan had begged her mom for an introduction, and this was it.

Eager to stake her claim before her older sisters, Dylan grabbed her Louis Vuitton and broke out of the Hummer.

"Wait!" Merri-Lee called. But Dylan couldn't be stopped. Her rejuvenated skin tightened from the cold New York air but there was no time to moisturize. Zachary was waiting and her pinkish tan was fading.

"Hello?" Dylan called bursting through the front door. "Zach?" she muttered, taken aback by legions of cameras and lighting rigs. *Were they filming this meet-and-greet the way*

Oprah filmed Twilight *fans when Robert Pattinson stopped by? Of course they were.* Daily Grind *fans loved watching other regular people being surprised.* Only Dylan was far from "regular" and her only surprise was a lack of Zach. Thick black cords curled into loops over the Italian marble floors, and booms and lights towered over her. Against the far wall stood a craft service table piled high with the foods Dylan hadn't seen in ten (minus six cheats) days, and crew members hustled about like they owned the place.

Merri-Lee appeared in the doorway. "Surprise!" She clapped.

Jaime and Ryan appeared beside her, their heavily made-up faces looking stunned. Lights popped on. Men lifted cameras onto their shoulders and aimed the lenses at their faces.

"What's going on?" Dylan asked, blinded.

"We have our own reality show called *Marvilous Marvils*!"

Dylan's forehead started to bead with sweat. Why had she eaten all six of those Luna Bars?

"That's why we had to leave town," Merri-Lee continued, through a bright smile. "The crew needed to wire the house while we wired our bodies." She winked at Dylan. "A ten-day cleanse to counteract the ten pounds the camera adds!"

Dylan turned to her sisters in amazement. They were grinning.

"We're gonna be stars!" Jaime exclaimed.

"The Kardashians are Kardashi-*out*!" Ryan added.

A loud bell rang. Dylan and Ryan jumped. Jaime screamed. The crew lowered their gear.

"Okay, gang, we're gonna take it from the top," a male voice announced over a PA system. "Dylan, this time without the Zach mention. Jaime, instead of 'stars,' can you say 'reality stars,' and Ryan, leave out the Kardashian comment—same network. Merri-Lee, you were perfect."

A tired-looking brunette in a black hoodie, black skinny jeans, and gray Converse ushered the Marvils back out the door.

After the director called "Action," Dylan entered the foyer again and yelled, "Hullo?"

And again.

And then again.

And another time after that.

After the final take, Dylan peeled off her faux-fur bomber jacket and raced for the food table. She was deciding between a plate of nachos and a baby carrot when a pale man with a walkie-talkie clipped to his jeans handed her a stack of papers.

"Here's your shoot schedule, miss," said the production assistant.

Dylan scanned the grid. *Ehma*-Emmy! They planned on using her *ah-lot*. She reached for the carrot and took a bite. She could practically hear Ryan and Guiliana scoring major gossip points about her on *E! News*.

Dylan grabbed her HTC Evo, a Christmas gift from her sisters. Wait until the PC heard about this! She was forming the perfect "Who's got red hair, her own reality show, and isn't Kathy Griffin?" text when the walkie-talkie guy grabbed her phone.

"'Scuse me?" Dylan said, her fist clenching.

He handed her another stack of papers thicker than September *Vogue*.

"Sign those. And if you're under eighteen your mom needs to sign, too."

"No need. I'm twenty-one."

"Cool," he said, unfazed.

"Wait! You actually believe I'm twenty-one?"

He shrugged. "I've been working on reality shows for three years. I don't know what to believe anymore."

Deflated, Dylan glanced at the papers. The header said CONFIDENTIALITY CONTRACT in all-caps. She winced at the memories of the last time she had needed to sign a confidentiality clause, when Merri-Lee had interviewed the (former) world champion tennis star Svetlana Slootskyia in Hawaii.

"Do I have to?" Dylan asked.

"Yes," Merri-Lee insisted, butting in. "And this is serious. You can't even tell your friends. They'll have to hear about it like everyone else, during my live New Year's Yves party!"

The pale guy added, "It's a legally binding document that will hold up in a court of law. If you violate it, the repercussions are severe."

"How severe?" Dylan wondered aloud. "Lindsay Lohan severe, or rest of the country severe?"

"Rest of the country," he assured her. "For starters you'll have to reimburse us for the cost of the show. Two million plus," he said before she had time to ask. "So be honest: Can you keep this secret?"

Dylan grabbed her phone from his hand. "Puh-lease!"

She managed to conceal six cheats during a ten-day juice fast. How much harder could this be?

"You know why his name is Bernie Madoff?" asked a silver-haired man in a blue suit and a crisp red tie.

Alicia took a small sip of sparkling water and waited for the punch line.

"Because he *made off* with everyone's money."

Her parents, Len and Nadia, seemed as amused as the other guests at their table. Alicia's laugh was faker than the *Hills* finale, but thankfully no one noticed.

This lunch was important. She had carefully selected a sophisticated, simple outfit for The 21 Club's annual Christmas lunch—a dark gray Ralph Lauren sweater that downplayed her C-cups and played up her pencil skirt. But judging by the flouncy cocktail dresses in the dining room, she'd made a mistake. She felt like one of the darts she'd thrown in Josh Hotz's game room: totally off the mark.

Every Christmas Day, Alicia and Nadia joined Len for a luncheon with his lawyer colleagues. It was a candlelit snoozefest, but Alicia was always rewarded for her attendance with an extra-special present afterward. Today, as they dined deep in the heart of Manhattan, their table and bellies stuffed with heavy meats and risotto, Alicia was hoping for some cardio-shopping on Fifth Avenue.

While Len began talking about his latest trial, Alicia fished her phone out of her Twelfth St. by Cynthia Vincent studded bag and checked to see if Massie had written her back. She'd texted the alpha when she'd arrived at The 21 Club with a 911 about whether her outfit was the right call. Massie had yet to respond.

Alicia thumbed through the rest of her inbox as talk of tort reform built around her. A message from Hermia, a name she hadn't seen in ages, stood out.

New Year, New Guidance! said the subject line. In the body of the message, surrounded by stars and moons, was text that read: *Let your celestial guru guide you on your journey into the new year with an e-reading. Limited-time cost of $75.*

Ever since she'd met the psychic at Merri-Lee's New Year's Yves party a few years ago, Alicia had been on Hermia's mailing list. Normally she would *ew*-schew psychics, but Hermia did predict the forming of the Pretty Committee. She even knew Claire would join them long before she moved to Westchester. If that wasn't worthy of an e-mail subscription, what was?

After a quick glance around the table and another perfunctory laugh, Alicia slouched in her velvet seat so that her hands—and her phone—were hidden under the white tablecloth. She connected to Hermia's site and scheduled an e-reading for ay-sap. It wasn't curiosity that drove her to withdraw seventy-five dollars from her PayPal account. It was boredom. A trip to the future was her only way out.

A chat box with an image of Hermia's serious gray eyes and grandma-white hair popped up.

You've done a good deal of traveling this year, Alicia. I see that it's taught you some valuable life lessons.

Alicia rolled her eyes. Dealing with her Spanish cousins and winning a spot in an ii! video last summer had only reinforced what she already knew: that she was hawt.

You are very good with physicality and movement. If you are not a dancer, become one, Hermia typed.

It didn't take a psychic to know she was the best student at the prestigious Body Alive Dance Studio.

"Tell me something I don't know," Alicia typed back.

An animated icon of Hermia began spinning. *Please wait while I decipher my vision of your future.*

Alicia returned to the present, where the conversation was still more *Law & Order* than Alice + Olivia.

Alicia, your prediction for the New Year is . . .

She held her breath.

You are going to rise up and become the leader of your group. Don't be afraid. It's time.

Ehma-huh? A shiver ran down Alicia's spine. What did *that* mean?

She thumbed a frustrated "????" to Hermia, but the psychic's icon had a bright red bar flashing diagonally across it. *You can hear more for another $75.*

Alicia was about to accept the terms and conditions when Nadia's Caliente Coral–clad fingers wrapped around Alicia's wrist like the Elizabeth and James tusk-link bracelet she had her eye on.

"Put the phone away," Nadia smile-demanded, making sure

the other guests never lost sight of her Rembrandt-enhanced teeth.

Alicia felt like her tongue had swollen to twice its normal size. She gathered up her shiny black hair and tried to discreetly fan the back of her neck, but Hermia's words were screaming on repeat in her head. *You're going to become the leader . . . leader . . . leader . . .*

"Denise, David," Nadia called across the table to Len's colleagues, "Did you know my daughter is an expert arguer? Perhaps we have a future lawyer on our hands!" They nodded and looked interested, but when it came to their conversation, Alicia felt like Angie and Brad. She just couldn't engage.

Instead, she tried to decipher what Hermia meant by leader of the group—maybe she meant *dance* group? But Alicia had been the leader of that ever since Skye Hamilton left for Alpha Academy.

Alicia fanned her pits. Past Alicia would have ah-dored a prediction like this. She spent so much of her life competing with Massie for alpha status. But Present Alicia didn't want it anymore. And she was pretty certain Future Alicia wouldn't either.

She shuddered, thinking back to when she had created the SoulM8s, OCD's first ever girl-boy clique, after the Pretty Committee had disbanded. It had been so much work being alpha—organizing, planning, brainstorming, and making sure everyone else was happy and having fun. It was *nawt* Alicia's idea of a good time. And it had almost cost her everything. No, Alicia hearted being Massie's beta.

It gave her all the prestige and none of the headaches.

If Hermia had been right about anything, it was that Alicia had learned a lot of valuable life lessons this year. The most valuable of all being: She would never be a social alpha again. No matter what some psychic thought her future held.

"If you don't tell me where were going, I'll never change my underwear again," Todd Lyons said.

"Any excuse to stay in those lucky Buzz Lightyear briefs," teased Judi Lyons from the front seat of the family Ford Taurus.

"But Mommmm," he whined, kicking the back of her seat.

"Patience, son," Jay admonished from behind the wheel. "We're almost there."

Claire tried to tune out her younger brother by savoring the chocolaty taste of love inside every one of her C&Cs— she'd rationed a small bag to take on the drive. While Todd continued to beg for clues, Claire inhaled the sugar-coated plastic smell of her candy pouch to mask the stench of the Old Spice body spray Todd had received in his Christmas stocking. It didn't work. She cracked the window, hoping a sliver of cold wind would suck out the fumes. But they had embedded themselves in the tan upholstery and held on tight. Mold Spice would have been a more accurate name.

Ping!

Claire checked her text messages.

Massie: Officially changing the name of this hell-i-day to ChristMISS because it sooo missed being fun. Can I crash at your house? I'm about to start carb-loading for warmth.

Claire: Sure. It's ur house ☺

Massie: Thx. Gonna start packing.

Claire wrinkled her brow. *Packing? For one night?*

Massie: BTW where R U?

Claire: No clue. ☺

Claire giggled as the Taurus made a sharp turn down a familiar block. Her father pulled the car over to the side of the road, and her mother turned around with a giddy gleam in her eye.

"Hey! This is Layne's street!" Claire said.

Todd bounced up and down in his seat. "Is this it? Are we getting our surprise here?"

Judi dangled two sleep masks in front of them. "Not just yet. You have to put these on first!"

"No way! They say most kidnappings are done by the parents!" Todd exclaimed.

"That's a chance you'll just have to take," Judi said, sliding the mask over her son's red hair.

"Did Layne put you up to this?" Claire asked, lowering the cold black silk over her eyes.

"Nope. Now zip it," Jay said, putting on his blinker and

easing back into the street. Claire felt like Jenna from *Pretty Little Liars*: She couldn't see a thing.

"I think we're going to get shot," Todd whispered.

"If anyone shoots you, it's gonna be me," Claire whispered back.

The Taurus slowed to a stop.

"No peeking," Judi warned, helping her children out of the car. Claire stepped onto a patch of frozen grass, her Target boots making a crunching noise. Though the sun was bright, it wasn't enough to counter the icy wind that whipped through her hair and bit her earlobes. Shivering, she wished she had on Todd's puffy jacket instead of the thin white satin–lined peacoat Massie handed down to Claire.

Claire tried to get her bearings. It sounded like kids were playing nearby. Someone was starting their car. A bike bell rang. Smells like wood burning fireplaces and Christmas turkey swirled around her. Claire inhaled them straight to her stomach. Scents and sounds like those, unless they were coming directly from the Blocks' house, didn't exist in the Blocks' neighborhood—the houses were too far apart. Her insides suddenly warmed.

Judi gripped Claire's shoulders and angled her left. "Ready?"

"Ready," Claire said, having absolutely no idea what to expect. She hadn't asked for anything special this Christmas.

"Surprise!" her parents shouted at the same time.

Claire and Todd removed their sleep masks.

Huh?

She was looking at a regular house. It was two stories with yellow siding and deep, country red doors and shutters. A two-car garage sat off to the right. The small front yard was covered in snow, but the tops of bushes stood proudly underneath the front windows. It wasn't big; it wasn't wrapped in blinking lights; and unless Claire was mistaken, it didn't belong to Mark Salling from *Glee*, and he wasn't inviting her over for a sing-along. So what was the big deal? Todd looked from one parent to the next, then settled on Claire with an expression of utter incomprehension.

"Surprise! It's our new house!" Judi and Jay said simultaneously, their faces bright with excitement, or maybe just the cold. "Merry Christmas!"

Shutthefrontdoor!

"*Seriously?*" Claire screamed like she had just met a Jonas brother and then threw her arms around her parents.

"Can we go in?" Todd asked, racing up the three steps to the porch.

"Not yet. We take possession Thursday," Jay explained. "Wait until you see the basement, though. There's enough room for a pool table *and* air hockey."

"What about a wrestling ring?" Todd jumped up and down in the snow. His jeans sagged, revealing the green elastic band of his lucky undies. Claire made a silent apology for doubting the briefs' powers. Who knew? Maybe they had something to do with this.

Claire couldn't help it; she screamed again. Their own house! Their own *adorable* house. On the same street as Layne! Close enough for Claire to ride her bike to OCD and the high school! A place where they could finally hang the "Lyons Live Here" sign that had been collecting dust in a still-unpacked box since they moved! A house that belonged to the Lyonses, instead of the Blocks.

The Blocks.

Claire's stomach jumped to its death as she thought about leaving Massie. Living in the guest house made her part of the PC. What was going to happen when Claire didn't live within *text-me-and-I'll-be-there-in-sixty-seconds* distance from her alpha? Would she still be invited to Friday night sleepovers? Could she still be a GLU if she was also a PASTE (Previously Allowed Someone who was Then Exiled)? And what about Massie? How could Claire abandon her on this hell-i-day?

Todd was already claiming the cluster of trees by the side yard so he and Tiny Nathan could build a fort. Jay and Judi were talking about a porch swing. Claire had never seen everyone in her family so happy at the same time. She wished she could bottle up that cheer and then give it to Massie like it was a Vitamin Water Zero.

Because like it or not, Claire and the Lyons family were moving out of the guest house and into the new house—and soon. Claire bit her lip and reached for another C&C, only to find her stash was gone.

Along with any hope that Massie could count on Claire.

Kristen stood shivering under a gray sky, surrounded by red-and-navy-clad all-stars. Inhaling the sharp biting air, she buried her fingers in the cuffs of her new red-and-navy Soccer Sisters windbreaker and braced herself for some rooftop drills. She, with some major help from her mom, had volunteered to host the Soccer Sisters' "Cleat & Greet" party that afternoon. But she hadn't been able to swallow a single pizza roll. Her insides seized up the minute they realized the strongest players in Westchester County were packed in her teeny living room.

Kristen shuffled her legs, then leaned down to adjust her shin guards. Hunched over, she raised her eyes and peeked at her new teammates.

Andrea Hart stood over to her left, stretching her hamstrings and popping orange gum. She was at least six feet tall, with leg muscles that looked more like wads than quads. Rumor was she had *Survivor*-like skills: She could outwit, outplay, and outlast every girl in the state.

To her right, a small group of girls were running drills. Jennifer Scholaski was French-braiding her hair while kicking a ball from one foot to the other. Kristen worried that the pizza rolls she hadn't eaten would still manage to find their way back up her throat if she watched Jennifer juggle for one more second. Jen was an all-star striker, and rumor had it that Division I schools were already scouting her. The two girls beside her were equally impressive with their unmistakable STARS bodies—Strong, Talented, Athletic, and Ready to Score.

Shake it off. No fear. Focus. Kristen straightened up and braced herself for another whistle. Like her coach and Ayn Rand always said: *Intimidation is a confession of intellectual impotence.*

"Soccer Sisters!" a gruff, hoarse yell came bubbling from the throat of Coach Blake. Short and squat, he had rhino leg muscles, a bald head, and a baby face.

"Line up for drills!" he called, and Kristen followed her sisters into formation.

You can do this, she told herself. She was used to drills. She could do them in heels and still beat the rest of her OCD teammates. But she wasn't standing beside her OCD teammates. She was standing *under* the Soccer Sisters—by at least three inches.She wasn't with the rest of her OCD teammates anymore—she was with the Soccer Sisters. Suddenly she felt very much like she imagined Justin Long had when he dated Drew Barrymore: totally out of her league.

"*Trap, dribble, kick,! Trap, dribble, kick!*" As Coach Blake barked out orders and the girls in front of her in line attacked the ball, Kristen surrendered. Maybe she would never have to break the news to the Pretty Committee. Maybe she wouldn't last past the Cleat & Greet. Maybe she was meant to be the big fish in the small OCD pond, rather than a small fish who was about to be gobbled up by a killer shark named Andrea.

Peep! Peeeeep!

Coach Blake's whistle pierced through the air again. "Gregory!"

It was her turn. As she faced Andrea, who stood in the makeshift goal, Kristen's brain shut down and her body took over, doing what it had been trained to do for the last nine years. As the black-and-white soccer ball left Coach Blake's hands and arced through the air, her green eyes narrowed. Time slowed. The honks of passing cars on the street below muted. The whoosh of the ball and the thump of her heartbeat were all she heard. *Somebody blot my face because it's time to shine!*

Her foot met the ball at the perfect angle, with just the right amount of strength, and sent it sailing across the rooftop. Her ponytail swished out behind her, her Soccer Sisters windbreaker crinkled, her skin buzzed. Kristen kept her eyes on the ball, anticipating the applause her teammates would give her when the ball shot into the net.

WHACK.

A collective gasp filled the rooftop.

Uh-oh.

Andrea gripped the ball against her stomach and doubled over. She fell to her knees. A sound more piercing that the coach's whistle rang through Kristen's ears. *Now what?* Remove her shin guards? Fold up her windbreaker? Pray that Andrea didn't buy into the whole eye-for-an-eye thing? No matter how risky, an apology was definitely in order.

Andrea wobble-stood and stomp-marched over to Kristen. The other girls stepped out of the way and formed a tight circle around them. Coach Blake took a passive step back. *Was he seriously going to let nature take its course? Because things die in nature all the time?*

"Gregory?" Andrea's voice boomed.

Kristen checked the roof for her mother. She wasn't there.

Andrea's blue eyes widened as she approached. She held out her hand and Kristen braced herself for a punch. Instead she got a slap on the back. A . . . friendly one. "Nice kick!"

"Really?" Kristen said, relaxing her shoulders.

"With Kristen, there's no way we can lose this season!" Jennifer shouted, and a cheer rose up. Even Coach Blake joined in. After a group hug, the coach demanded everyone get back to work.

The sharp wind bit at Kristen's nose. Coach's shrill whistle poked her eardrums like someone was stabbing her with an icicle. And her body was trembling with hunger.

Yet Kristen had never felt better.

Massie surveyed her bedroom, trying to remember what it looked like before it was littered with half-filled boxes, messy piles of tunics, and last season's skinny jeans. She squinted, ignoring Kendra's wrinkle-prevention mantra—"a squint at thirteen makes a grown woman scream"—but it was no use. No matter how much she tried to trick her eyes, she couldn't block out the events of the past two weeks. The destruction of her life stood before her like the torn-apart Macy's juniors section during its Day-After-Christmas Sale.

Bean was comfortably perched in a Barneys boot box awaiting the big move across the backyard. She was wearing a festive red-and-silver outfit that Landon's pug, Bark Obama, had sent her as a Christmas gift.

"Should we bring the Massiequin: yea or nay?"

Bean barked once, and Massie nodded. "Ah-greed. We both know Kuh-laire could use her more than I could." Massie made a check mark on the Smart Board she'd rolled in from her father's office, which she was using to organize her move. So far, all it said was *Winter and Resort Wear* and *Stuff to Spruce Up Kuh-laire and Massie's Bedroom*.

The sounds of Ke$ha's latest song rang out from somewhere on Massie's bed, and she rifled through a pile of scarves to find her iPhone. Dylan had programmed in the ringtone, declaring that Ke$ha was the only musician on today's scene who "got" her energy. Massie thought all Ke$ha "got" was bad makeup advice.

"Mass! Where have you been? You haven't picked up in days!"

"How was your trip? Was it ah-mazing?" Massie asked. As soon as the words were out, she regretted them. Because now Dylan would have to ask a similar question in return—and Massie did *nawt* want to tell Dylan how her Christmas was going. In fact, she would need years of sessions with therapists and Scarlett Johansson's acting coach before she'd be able to talk about this Christmas without crying.

"It was good. I lost major water weight and mostly hung by the beach. You?"

"Same," Massie managed. "Without the beach part."

They were both silent. Massie searched for something to say but couldn't think of a single topic. Everything on her mind was off-limits to everyone but Claire.

"Question," Dylan finally said. "Have you ever had a huh-*yuge* secret that you wanted to tell but couldn't?"

Massie felt like she'd swallowed a candy cane sideways. Had Dylan heard about her financial fallout? Were people talking about it? Did Merri-Lee want to run a riches-to-rags story on the Blocks?!

". . . Sometimes your family's not enough. You need to talk about it with your friends, right? . . ."

Dylan was still chattering on about secrets and lies but Massie could barely hear her anymore.

". . . What if someone accidentally blabs and word gets out . . ."

"Hullo?" Massie blurted. "Dylan, can you hear me? Hullo?"

"Yeah, I can hear you," Dylan said. "Can you hear me?"

"Hullo? Dyl? Are you there?"

"Massie! I can hear you. Can you hear me?"

"Dyl?"

"Mass?"

"Dyl?"

"Mass!"

"Ugh, AT&T." Massie groaned and then hung up. Dylan had left her no choice. She was getting too close, no doubt searching for a confession.

Massie collapsed on a Lanvin batwing cardigan that still had tags dangling from the label. She refused to look at the price. It would only make her cry.

Kendra knocked on the open door.

"If you're not coming to shoot me, go away."

"Massie, I'd like you to meet Tamara Hardwood."

"Who?" Massie sat up.

"Our realtor." Kendra smiled apologetically at a well-preserved brunette in a fitted black blazer and matching skirt. "She was kind enough to stop by on the holiday weekend. Isn't that so great of her?"

Realtor?

"It's no biggie." Tamara waved away the praise. "I'm Jewish."

Massie stood. The room seemed to tighten along with her throat. "Isn't today the Sabbath?"

"Oh, it's okay. I'm not observant," Tamara smiled widely.

"Uh, clearly," Massie murmur-muttered. If she was, she would have known Massie was talking about religion, not some random character trait.

"I'm showing Tamara around the estate," Kendra explained. Her eyes roamed across Massie's room, landing on the boxes and clothes and stray boots littering every surface.

"It's such a spectacular home," Tamara added. "And this room? *Gorge.*" Suddenly she was all business. "Before we list I'll stage it, of course. Something in a warmer palette. White doesn't exactly scream cozy." She winked at Massie. And then to Kendra she said, "Don't worry. A few coats of paint and the place will sell itself. Even in this bear economy."

Sell?

Kendra sigh-nodded.

Tamara turned to Massie and pasting a big smile on her unevenly lined lips. "I know one girl who's ready to say good-bye to this room."

"'Scuse me?"

Tamara gestured to the boxes and tapped on the Smart Board. "It looks like you're excited about the big move!"

"Big move?" Massie asked, heart pounding. "You mean to Claire's?"

"Tamara, why don't I show you the rest of the house," Kendra suggested, steering the realtor toward the hall.

As Tamara inspected the doorframe, Massie glared at her mother. She felt like Bristol Palin while Levi Johnston was pitching reality shows in Hollywood: totally left in the cold.

Dylan tried blinking but it was impossible. Her eyes wouldn't budge. She struggled to sit up, but that, too, proved futile. A pair of strong arms held her against the massage table in Merri-Lee's spa bathroom. She was stuck.

Nicolette, the network's aesthetician, playfully swatted at Dylan's arm. At least, Dylan thought it was a playful swat. But with her eyes taped shut, she couldn't be sure.

She was sure of one thing, though: Attaching eyelash extensions took longer than growing them from scratch.

"Stop moving," Nicolette demanded, her Tic-Tac-scented breath slithering up Dylan's nostrils and cooling her brain.

Dylan felt something dangerously sharp touching down on her lid and then a gentle tugging of her upper lash line. Blindness was so not fun. She flashed back to a history class about the various methods of torture enacted upon prisoners during the Middle Ages. She'd be willing to bet her hefty *Marvilous Marvils* paychecks that remaining still while getting eyelash extensions topped the list.

"Can I at least make another phone call?"

"If it keeps you from complaining, I'll dial the numbers myself," Nicolette said gamely.

"How about someone with Sprint this time. AT&T to

AT&T drops more than Beyoncé drops singles. Try Alicia."

Alicia's dad was a hotshot lawyer. Maybe he'd be able to help her sidestep the confidentiality situation.

Nicolette held the phone against Dylan's ear.

"Heyyy," Alicia said, after two rings. "Merry Christmas! How are you? Are you back? How was the Caribbean?"

"Caribbean-y . . ." she joked, not wanting to talk about her ten-day cleanse, but rather the fastest way to cleanse her soul of the secret she was carrying. "So, Leesh, question: What would you do if you were sworn to secrecy about something but wanted to tell?"

"Same thing I always do: run a gossip points cost-benefit analysis. If the gossip points are bigger than the trouble I might get in for telling, I risk it. If not, I don't."

Dylan pressed the phone to her lips and whispered, "This is more serious than gossip points. People could go to jail for telling."

Alicia was quiet.

"Hullo?" Dylan said, shaking her phone. "Not again. Gawd, I hate AT&T. Leesh, are you there?"

"Yeah, I'm here. Sorry, I was just thinking."

"And?"

"And this is a question for an alpha. Not me. Ask Massie."

"I'm thought you could help because your dad—"

"Hold on, Dylan," Alicia said. "What, Mom?" she called. "*Dinner?*"

Now? Dylan couldn't open her taped eyes to check the time

but the trace of balsamic in her burps meant only one thing: Lunch was still digesting.

"I have to go," Alicia said. "Mom freaks when the paella is cold."

"But—"

The line went dead.

When did Alicia start choosing carbs over gossip?

"Nicolette?" Dylan said, lifting her phone over her head. It smashed up against something hard.

"*Ouch!* My chin!"

"Sorry. Would you please dial Kristen?"

The aesthetician jammed the ringing phone against Dylan's ear so hard the post of Dylan's diamond stud almost shattered her skull. She was about to scream when—

"Okay, how tan are you on a scale from Claire to Alicia?"

"I'm about a Kristen after a full day at Massie's pool, SPF four."

"Nice." She giggled.

"Listen, Kristen, I need some advice and my battery's about to die so . . ."

"Sure, what's up?"

"What would you do if you had a big secret—like, really huh-yuge—but you were obligated to keep it quiet even though you were dying to tell someone?"

"Ahem," a male voice said over her, his breath smelling like salsa. "I couldn't help but overhear your conversation just now."

"Who is that?" Kristen asked. "Are you visiting your dad?"

Dylan thumbed around for the END button and disconnected the call.

"I hope you're not in breach of the confidentiality contract." Dylan recognized the voice. It was the mysterious producer who always shouted "Back to one" and "Let's try that again!" over the PA system. Dylan fought to catch a glimpse of him, but her lids were no match for the super-stick grip of Nicolette's tape.

"Who, me?" Dylan asked, wondering how one feigned shock without the use of her eyes. "No. I was running lines with my drama partner. We're doing *Secret Life of Bees* and, um, I play the bee with the secret."

"Well, in the end, I hope your bee decides to keep the secret, or the whole hive will come crashing down on her," he said with a final blast of salsa.

"Don't worry." Dylan forced a smile.

Of course, if the hive didn't crush her, the weight of this secret surely would.

Claire's room had become a "before" scene in an episode of *Hoarders*. Claire brushed aside her bangs, opened her closet door, and began pulling clothes. There was already a big lump of "donate before the PC finds out I wore these," a small mound of "could wear while studying," and a midsized pile of "new house–worthy." But there was still so much to do. How was she supposed to get it all packed and organized in less than a week?

Massie burst into Claire's room with a box of her own. Her amber eyes, red and watery, took in the chaos. "Kuh-laire, it's so ah-dorable of you to get rid of your ugly things to make room for my cute ones." She kicked aside a PowerPuff Girls nightgown. "Just for that I grant you complete wardrobe access. It's a good thing I'm moving in."

"Moving in?" Claire screeched. "I thought you were just sleeping over. You know, tonight."

"Puh-lease. Look outside." Massie led her to the window. A baggage claim's worth of luggage sat on the lawn outside the guesthouse. "Would I bring all of that for one night?"

Claire managed to smile. "Probably."

"Isn't that why you're cleaning out your closets?"

"Of course," Claire lied, nervously tugging on the zipper of her light blue hoodie. "Why else would I be doing all of this?"

How could she possibly tell Massie she'd be abandoning her in her greatest moment of need? The girl looked more fragile than those wide-eyed Precious Moments figurines Grandma Lyons collected.

"Question for you," Massie began, gripping Claire with the intensity of her glare. "Any chance you told Dylan about my . . ." She hesitated, as if her next words might detonate and trigger an explosion. ". . . my *secret*?"

"No!" Claire crossed her fingers over her heart, twice. "I swear."

Massie cocked her head.

"Swear on your life?"

Claire lifted her palm. "Swear on my life."

"Your mom's life?"

"Swear."

"Dad's?"

"Swear."

"Todd's?"

"Easy. Swear," she joked, but Massie still wasn't convinced.

"What about . . ." Massie tapped her chin, looked up, and then swooped her glare back down for what she obviously assumed was the billion-dollar question. "What about *Cam's*?"

"Swear."

"Say it."

"I swear."

"All of it."

"I swear on Cam's life I did not tell Dylan, or anyone, about your secret."

"The money one."

"The money one." Claire sat on the edge of her bed. "I'm almost offended that you think I would tell."

"Um, are you a busboy?"

"No," Claire said.

"Then why are you turning the tables?" Massie asked.

"I—"

"That was about me not you. But I believe you now, so let's move on."

Claire sighed. She wanted to be there for Massie like Selena was there for Demi, but it was hard when she had her own secret to keep.

"Hey, Mass . . ." Claire wondered aloud. "Do you think we'd still be friends if we didn't live on the same estate?"

Massie did a belly-first dive onto Claire's bed, knocking the "maybe" pile of clothes onto the floor. "Oh, you don't have to worry about that, Kuh-laire!"

Claire felt the knot in her stomach unravel a little.

"Your family will never leave. Which is actually perfect because if mine does—not that they are, but they might . . . someday—I'll move in with you, keep the same address, and no one will know the difference!" she declared, her eyes brightening. "It'll be our secret."

Another one?

Claire knew she had to tell Massie the truth and ask point-blank if they'd still be friends once they didn't live together. And even if Massie pulled a Simon Cowell and left, at least Claire would know the truth and all the secrets would be over.

"This is cute for you," Massie said to a gray Alexander Wang tee shirt. "Keep this one."

"You gave it to me," Claire admitted.

"Oh." Massie giggled. "Ooops." Her smile was endearing, a mix of warmth and vulnerability. It stuck with Claire like a sad movie.

"Maybe you should tell them," Claire tried. "See what happens."

"Opposite of great idea," Massie said, picking through Claire's old blouses. "'See what happens' is for ordering jeans online, not for telling your friends you're *poor*." She reached for her necklace and dragged the black diamond along the chain.

"Did you get that for Christmas?" Claire asked innocently.

Massie nodded yes.

"Then you're not *poor*."

"Tell that to the frozen fish tank in my dad's study. We're selling it to a sushi chef from Ichi San."

Claire crossed the room and joined Massie on her bed, gently moving the "for keeps" clothes to her desk chair. "The point is, friends are there for each other no matter what. Did you bail on Kristen when you found out she wasn't rich?"

Massie paused to consider this. "Interesting point. Run with it."

Empowered, Claire sat taller. "It's just that you've been there for them so many times . . ."

"Name ten," Massie said, as if the alpha's greatest hits just slipped her mind. "Not including the one you just said."

"Okay, ten . . ." Claire thought hard. "Keep in mind I've only been here a year."

"Ten."

She stood and began pacing. "One. You helped Alicia buy her first minimizing bra. Two, you supply Kristen with new outfits every morning before school. Three, you designed their dirty devils Halloween costumes. Four, you had Jakob fix my bangs after Layne butchered them when I was trying to be Old-Claire for Cam. Four, you helped Dylan when Mr. Myner was dating her mom. Five, you formed the NPC after OCD became BOCD! Six, you started an underground clinic to teach lip virgins how to kiss. Um . . ." She searched the sticky corners of her mind for more. "Okay seven."

"You skipped seven."

"Seven, you turned the overflow trailers into Tiffany's boxes so they wouldn't feel like losers. Eight, you hosted billions of sleepovers—and spa days—so that's eight. Nine, you sawed off Nina's heels when she stole our crushes. And ten . . . " *Come on, Claire, don't choke now . . . you're almost there . . .*

Massie sat cross-legged on the bed, folded her arms across her chest, and glared expectantly.

"Ten. You introduced them to me," Claire said with a playful smile.

Massie arched her brows.

"My bangs and Keds made them feel better about their own hair and shoes. So you helped boost their confidence."

"Kuh-laire, are you a ballerina?"

"Why?" she snapped, angry at herself for even bothering. "Because I'm so *leotarded*? Or because I'm a *tulle*?"

"No." Massie jumped to her feet, "Because you're so on pointe!"

"I am?"

"I've been an ah-mazing friend!" The light had returned to her friend's amber eyes. "Don't poor people always say that's worth more than all the money in the world?"

Claire nodded enthusiastically.

"And poor people would know that better than anyone, right? I mean, it's not like they can afford cable or magazines or computers. They probably huddle around an open oven and analyze this kind of stuff for fun."

Did she honestly believe that? Not that Claire would ever ask. Challenging Massie while she was boosting herself was like waking a sleepwalker: It could lead to danger.

"Gawd, you are so right . . ." Massie began texting, her fingers flying over the touch screen with a renewed sense of purpose.

Massie: 911! Meet at GLU HQ 2-moro at 11.

She hit send. Claire was the first to respond.

Claire: Can't wait. C U then.

And then:

Alicia: Whatever u say! Ur the alpha. Always have been always will B ☺

Dylan: Major family day. I can probably get away for 15 but no more.

Kristen: Can't stay long. Soccer thing @ 11:30.

"*Ehmagawd!*" Massie threw her iPhone on Claire's bed like it had been sprayed with Todd-snot. "The poor people were wrong! They know that I'm not rich, and they're over me!"

"Do you seriously think they like you for your money?"

"You tell me!" Massie snapped, waving her phone in Claire's face. "You're the alpha?" she spat. "Alicia is ah-bviously mocking me! Dylan just spent ten days with her family! That's more back-to-back family time than they've had the last five years combined. And Kristen? A soccer thing during December break? *Puh-lease.* Change your name to Jesse James and lie to me again!" She smashed Claire's tasseled pillow into her face and groaned.

Claire searched her mind for a reasonable explanation for the Pretty Committee's flakiness but found nothing. Dylan *never* hung out with her family. Alicia *never* acknowledged her beta status. And Massie was right: What kind of crazy-intense team practices over Christmas break? What if Massie was right? What if the PC was breaking up with her now that her family was broke? And if they were so willing to dump a no-money Massie, there was zero hope for an off-estate Claire.

But were the girls really that callous? Had their friendships been that superficial? It wasn't possible. Even for them. Right?

Claire snuck a gummy. But even the sweet candy couldn't wash away the sour taste in her mouth.

Massie was more stiff than the marble statue Sotheby's had just removed from her front yard. She was standing in the center of the Blocks' barn-turned-spa-turned-cold-spa while Alicia, Kristen, and Dylan avoided her gaze. As a result, she avoided Claire's gaze because this whole stupid thing was her idea in the first place. Not that Claire noticed. She was biting her nails like they were made of sugar. Alicia was petting Bean, Dylan kept checking her phone, and Kristen was nervously rolling her foot back and forth on a soccer ball—like that would somehow convince Massie that her bogus story was true. The alpha wanted to scream, but could only manage a yawn.

Last night Claire had slept peacefully in a sleeping bag on the floor, while Massie had tossed and turned in her foam-filled comforter. The white numbers on her iPhone had flitted by, like they were counting down to Massie's execution. Just as the French peasants had lopped off Marie Antoinette's head over cake, the Pretty Committee were about to ax her over dough.

"So what's going on?" Alicia finally asked. "Is this an intervention? Did I do something?"

"*You?*" Kristen said. "I thought everyone was mad at me."

"No one's mad at anyone," Massie managed. *Yet.*

"Phew." Dylan wiped her forehead, "I thought it was me."

"Like maybe we were *lashing* out at you?" Alicia teased.

Dylan giggled. "We got them on our vacation." She blinked. "You like?"

"You better be careful crossing the street, Bambi," Kristen cackled. "If you see headlights, look down."

Claire shot Massie a *tell-them* glare. Massie shot back a *Kuh-laire-are-you-a-JanSport-then-get-off-my-back* glare.

Still, she pressed on. "I wanted to let you know—" Massie paused to scoop up Bean and took a long whiff of puppy smell. The pug licked her back. *Why couldn't everyone be this loyal?*

Eight eyeballs were fixed on her. Waiting . . . wondering . . . Her future hung in the balance of their blinking lashes. And Massie wasn't so confident on the brightness of said future. Because for every one of the great things she had done for them, there was a not-so-great-thing she had also kinda done.

She hadn't let Claire be a Dirty Devil.

She'd kept Alicia out of the *TeenVogue* photo shoot (although Alicia had deserved it for cheating on the OCD uniform contest).

She'd called Alicia "Fannish." Ah-lot.

She'd told Dylan that burping was gah-ross.

She'd made her friends dump their crushes during the boyfast.

She'd kicked everyone out of the PC at least once.

She'd tried to keep Dylan and Derrington apart.

She'd tried to keep Dempsey and Kristen apart.

She'd Lycra'd her friends way more than ten times . . .

"Mass, I don't mean to rush you but I have to get going," Dylan said, texting.

"Same," Kristen added, toe-flicking her ball and catching it.

"Fine," Massie said with an *it's-now-or-never* exhale. "Here's the thing. Itturnsoutmydadlostalotofmoneythanksto-theeconomy." The girls exchanged glances but Massie kept projectile-vomiting the truth, hoping to feel lighter in the end. "That'swhythehouseiscoldthat'swhyIgotyoumakeupsamples-forChristmasandthat'swhywe'llbemovingtoasmallerestate. So that'sitthat'swhatIwantedtosay." For some reason she ended with an awkward curtsy.

Claire applauded. Kristen opened and closed her mouth like a trout. Dylan and Alicia covered their lips with their holiday-polished fingertips. Massie looked sadly down at her own. They were chipped and broken. Just like her spirit.

Massie scuffed her Frye boots on the wood floor, expecting her soon-to-be-ex-friends to whip out their phones. Her breaking news was worth at least 10,000,000 Gossip Points. Life as she knew it was officially over.

Ehmagawd, somebody say something!

"Well, I just thought you deserved to hear it from me," she finally mumbled. "You can all go to your family things and your soccer whatevers. Thanks for listening."

But then Claire reached for Kristen's hand. Kristen grabbed Alicia's. And Alicia took Dylan's. Suddenly, like a runaway game of Red Rover, they charged toward their alpha and enveloped her in a Pretty Committee perfume-scented cloud of love. A mix of Angel, sweaty soccer jersey, maple syrup, and salsa. Massie wanted to bottle it and name it: *Unconditional.*

Step aside, Beyoncé. There's a new Survivor in town.

CURRENT STATE OF THE UNION

IN	OUT
Low budget	No budget
Supportive friends	Supportive bras
Massie Broke	Massie Block

"Stripes?" Kristen suggested.

"On New Year's *Eve*?" Massie asked.

"Metallic?" Claire tried.

Massie wrinkled her nose. "Too last year."

"All-black?" Alicia suggested.

"Too Kelly Cutrone," Massie decided.

"Ruffles?"

"Too Kelly Osbourne."

"Hair extensions?"

"Too Kelly Clarkson."

A month ago, Massie's dismissiveness would have outraged Alicia, but today she was so alpha-appreciative she just lifted her finger and said, "Point."

"How about an ocean theme—greens and blues for everyone?" Dylan said. She blinked, and then pried the lashes on her right eye apart.

As Alicia sipped her sparkling water and half-listened to the other girls talk about what to wear to Merri-Lee's annual New Year's Yves party, she studied the redhead. There was something different about her—aside from the lens-dusters and shed water weight. It was almost like . . . she was hiding something.

61

When Alicia offered to have her driver, New Isaac (because Old Isaac was gone and they couldn't remember this guy's name) pick up the girls, Dylan shut her down. Something about how she'd get there on her own because they were doing construction on her street and there would be nowhere for them to stop. But New Isaac had passed by Magnolia Lane earlier that day and said the road was clear as crystal.

Kristen took a quick inventory of Alicia's walk-in closet. "What if we do a clothes swap? Claire wears something of mine, I wear something of Alicia's, Alicia wears something of Dylan's, and Massie—"

"Wears something of Kuh-laire's? *Ehma-never!*"

"No way would my C-cups fit into Dylan's A-cup shirts," Alicia pointed out.

"They're B's," Dylan insisted, unbuttoning the second button on her plaid shirt.

"Well, they B looking like A's," Alicia teased.

Everyone laughed but Massie. Her smile was falling dangerously close to a frown. Claire seemed to notice, too, and jumped in. "I really think we can pull a Tim Gunn on this and make it work."

But Massie just shook her head and flopped onto a ruby-colored beanbag. "It's hopeless. I can't pretend anymore. I don't want to wear someone's old clothes! It's New Year's Eve. Besides, it's a bad omen to wear something that's already been worn that night. It means you'll be wearing used clothes for the rest of the year!" She curled into fetal position and whined, "I have to shop."

Alicia suddenly felt guilty for wearing her brand-new ivory Ralph Lauren sweater dress and fringed Minnetonka boots. Massie looked just as current in her shimmery peach Alice + Olivia top and olive J Brands. Still, the beta understood. Who didn't like a week's worth of new clothes around the holidays? Even Claire and Kristen went trolling for hand-me-downs this time of year.

"I have a brill idea!" Alicia announced. "Why don't I sell my soon-to-be-so-last-year wardrobe? The LBRs will love it! I'll donate the cash to Massie so she can buy a New Year's Yves outfit. My dad's been looking for tax write-offs—whatever those are—but I think they have something to do with charity donations—"

Massie gasped.

"Ehmagawd, not that *you're* charity," Alicia tried, her tongue folding up like a drawbridge. "I just meant—"

"I think it's a great idea!" Claire interjected. "I have tons of stuff to sell."

Everyone giggled.

"What?" Claire asked, turning red. "If people think it's yours they'll buy it."

"Point," Alicia said, considering this. "But then they'll think it's mine."

Dylan burst out laughing. "I'll donate, too."

"I'll work the register," Kristen offered.

Massie stood and joined the girls on Alicia's bed. "I bet we could style some of Claire's old things to make them look cool. It *is* LBRs who we're *targeting*—no pun intended."

"Yay!" Alicia beamed at the round of love they were giving her idea. "Mass, you should come up with a list of jobs for us, a schedule, and a marketing plan. And I'll get my clothes and—"

"Um, Leesh, do I look like Lady Gaga's head?"

"No," Alicia mumbled.

"Then why are you making me the bigwig?"

Alicia's heart began to rev. "You're the alpha so I assumed—"

"Exactly. If LBRs see me selling clothes, they'll know something's up."

Alicia looked to Kristen. "Do you want to run it?"

"I wish I could but I have soccer stuff," she said, flexing her calves.

"Dylan, how about you?"

Dylan blinked her long lashes as she sneaked a peek at her iPhone. "I'm on—I mean, my mom's got a lot to do for the New Year's Yves show and she needs my help, so . . ."

Alice narrowed her eyes. "Since when does your mom ask you for help?"

Dylan's cheeks reddened under her freckles. "I'll contribute all my clothes, though."

"Kuh-laire?"

"I have to pack," she said, avoiding Alicia's dark eyes.

"You know, because Massie needs room for her stuff and everything."

"Why don't you do it, Leesh?" Massie suggested in a way that sounded more like insisting. "It *was* your idea."

"I guess I could," Alicia said, over the alpha-alert ringing in her ears. If she succeeded, she might be given more alpha duties and Hermia's prediction would start coming true. If she failed, she would be a failure. The situation couldn't have been more lose-lose than if it was Jillian Michaels's résumé.

Memories of the dinner party she'd organized for the SoulM8s danced in front of her like reflections in the mirror-lined walls at BADSS. The boys turning up their noses at her famous-couples-costume idea. Derrington wiggling his butt when she tried to engage them in sophisticated conversation. Dylan burping through the appetizers. Massie upstaging the whole thing with an ah-some fashion show in her backyard . . .

With each memory, Alicia's neck grew hotter, her pits sweatier, and her tongue thicker. It was almost like she was having an allergic reaction—to being an alpha.

"I have to pee," Alicia said, hurrying for her bathroom. Once inside, she leaned over the waterfall sink and splashed cool water on her face. Why was the universe suddenly intent on beta-blocking her?

Alicia pulled her phone from the inside of her moccasin and checked her daily horoscope on Hermia's website.

"You miss some of what you try for, and all of what you don't."

She read it and reread it, hoping it might morph into something different if she just stuck with it. But the prediction didn't change. It stood by its word, leaving Alicia with no choice but to do the same.

"Next stop: Marshalls!" Kristen cried from the front seat of her mom's Ford Focus. "You'll love it, Massie. It's my middle-class mecca."

"Target is mine," Claire chimed in from behind the driver's seat. She rustled the big Target bag at her feet lovingly. Where else could one purchase deodorant and designer-done-cheap? Next to her, Massie sighed audibly. Claire patted her on the shoulder. She knew this was hard for her friend, and she was impressed how reasonable she was being about it all. Massie was set for New Year's, but she still had 364 other days to consider, which is where Kristen and Claire came in.

They'd already hit Target, and though Massie's face had grown longer than the time between Jessica Simpson's recording contracts as they'd traipsed through the aisles, she had bought the gray scarf she was now donning. So what if she was wearing it as a disguise? It was still progress.

Claire eyed Massie. The alpha had done her best to make sure she still didn't *look* middle-class. She was wearing a new-ish pair of Earnest Sewn skinny jeans tucked into a pair of suede booties that Claire couldn't imagine walking in. Her belted wool coat was hanging open, showing a flash of bright green from a cashmere tank she wore under a fitted Theory

67

blazer. She'd pulled her hair back into a tight bun, wrapped the gray scarf around it, and wore big black Dior sunglasses, even though the sun was hidden behind a sheet of gray clouds. She obviously didn't want to be recognized.

"Thanks for driving us, Mrs. Gregory," Claire said.

Marsha smiled, turning a sharp left that made Claire's bangs fly up. "It's the least I could do after all the times Massie has given Kristen a ride. Where is Isaac, anyway? Has he been sick?"

The only sounds came from the radio. Claire normally loved holiday music, but once Christmas was over, it felt staler than neglected fruitcake.

"He's on vacation," Massie finally answered.

"Visiting family?" Ms. Gregory pressed.

"Yup," she said, turning to the window.

The sound of Kristen pulling her hoodie zipper up and down filled the silence. Marsha hummed along to the radio. Claire's phone buzzed with a new text.

Massie: Please tell me no one we know will be at Marshmallows.

Claire stifled a giggle. She could hear Kristen thumbing a response from the front seat.

Kristen: Operation middle-class makeover is officially under way!
Massie: Ugh.

Claire: Cheap . . . [she quickly deleted the word in favor of a more appealing one] Affordable clothes r cute! u'll see.

Kristen: Style is style, no matter the budget.

That seemed to please Massie because she put down her phone and swiped her lips with Chai Latte–flavored Glossip Girl, signaling that she was ready.

Kristen's mother pulled into a parking spot and everyone tumbled out of the Focus, except for Massie, who stopped to read a text.

Claire peered over her shoulder. Landon had sent her a picture message of a pair of bare feet half-buried in white sand, with the outline of a sea creeping toward him and a bottle of Vitamin Water at his feet.

Landon: Here's what I'm doing right now in Bali. You?

Massie removed her scarf and coat. She spread the scarf over the car seat and then propped herself up on her shoulders as if she had been casually resting upon it the whole time.

Kristen knocked on the car window. "You coming?"

"Just a sec." She pulled off her sunglasses, undid her bun, and re-glossed. Then she hit a button and the window rolled down. She handed Claire her iPhone. "Can you take a shot of me? Shoulders up. No car interior. Go!"

Claire exchanged a quick, confused glance with Kristen but then shrugged and snapped the image. Massie's face transformed into the sunny embodiment of girl-without-a-care-in-the-world. It was a great pic, if Claire said so herself. She couldn't wait to show Cam how she'd used the angle to make Massie's neck appear longer.

Massie took the phone and sent it to Landon with a message: *Spa day*.

Sometimes it amazed Claire how easily deception came to Massie. Or rather, how hard she was willing to work at making it look easy. Instead of pitying or judging her, Claire admired her. There was no one else like Massie Block. No matter how much she had—or didn't have—she could always be counted on to make a regular day memorable.

"Let's go." Claire smiled, hooking her arm in Massie's and leading her to Marshalls.

"Ehma-blind." Massie recoiled when the fluorescent lights hit her in the face. "This place is lit like Seven-Eleven."

Kristen rolled her eyes. "You get used to it. Shoes are to the left and straight ahead is the juniors department." She led Massie and Claire down the main aisle while Mrs. Gregory headed over to the housewares section.

"Everything's bunched together." Massie looked helplessly at Claire. "The fabrics can't breathe." Her face was pinched, like she was about to cry.

"Poly-blends don't need to breathe," Kristen explained patiently. "They're special that way."

"Oh," Massie said, cautiously reaching for a gold sweater and then snatching her hand back like it had nipped her flesh. "It's so . . . shiny! Like it's been sprayed with pesticides."

Claire shrugged. "You'll get used to it."

"Gawd, I hope not." Massie stroked her forearms as if to say, *I'll never let you suffer like that.*

Claire pointed at an accessories rack. "Look at those belts."

"Hmmmm." Massie wandered over to a wide black belt and rubbed it between her fingers. "Ehma-puh-leather! It's not even real!" She let go, and it wriggled down to the scuffed linoleum floor.

Claire reached into her tote and pulled out her depleted bag of C&Cs. "Anyone want one?"

"What are C&Cs?" Kristen asked, waving away the sugar treat.

"Claire and Cams." She blushed. "Part of my Christmas gift."

"What else did he get you?" Massie asked.

Claire couldn't believe she had kept the rest of his gift so quiet. But she couldn't find the right way to tell her friends that the new photography class meant she'd be late to every GLU sleepover. Assuming she'd even be included once they moved apart. "He sang me a song," she said, downplaying the *awwww* factor so they'd lose interest and change the subject.

"How ah-dorable," Kristen said to a red corduroy blazer. She whipped off her tweed toggle coat and handed it to Claire so she could try it on. "Mirror?" she asked. Claire pointed halfway down the aisle, and she took off. "Mass, what do you think? Cute over a hoodie, right?" Kristen straightened the cuffs.

"I'll be the judge of that," Massie said, hurrying toward her.

Claire stood back and watched them scrutinize the blazer. Clothes were fine, and shopping was fun because it meant hanging out with friends. But she couldn't imagine breaking down the pros and cons of anything unless it had to do with risky surgery or going to war.

She readjusted Kristen's coat in her arms, and something fell from a pocket and landed on the floor. All she could make out was an official-looking letter with an embossed soccer ball. Claire wondered if it had anything to do with her mysterious soccer commitments. Unfolding it was the only way to know for sure. And that was immoral.

But what if the fluorescent lights happen to catch it just the right way as Claire was returning it to the coat and she happened to see through the paper? Not as bad, right?

She bent to retrieve the piece of paper and surreptitiously held it up to the light. Several words stuck out: *"Soccer Sisters"* . . . *"Daily practices"* . . . *"Saturday morning games."* Claire's brows furrowed. Had Kristen been accepted to some soccer team?

"I'll take that," Kristen said, coming up behind Claire and grabbing the letter.

"Oh, it fell out," Claire said, expecting an explanation. But all she got was a red-cheeked explanation about how Kristen always found old junk in her pockets.

Claire blinked at Kristen, then cleared her throat. The piece of paper wasn't old junk. It had a date on it . . . from four days ago. Their eyes met in a gaze that was more charged than Massie's old credit cards.

Was Kristen keeping a secret, too?

"*Ehma*-finally!" Massie's screech startled Claire. She and Kristen turned to find their friend triumphantly holding up a pair of BCBG booties. "They're from this season. And they're 50 percent off!"

The girls applauded her find.

She shoved them into Claire's hands, along with a fistful of crumpled bills. "Can you puh-lease pay?" She wrapped her scarf back around her head and lowered her Dior sunglasses before glancing furtively around the store. "I'm not quite ready for *purchasing*."

With a sigh, Claire agreed. Operation middle-class makeover was progressing, even if it was only by one BCBG bootie step at a time.

"Hello, sweetie!" Merri-Lee cried, like she wasn't even mad Dylan was thirty-five minutes late for call time. She leaned forward and kissed her daughter on the forehead and then ushered her inside.

"Um . . . hi, Mom!" Dylan's red curls got caught in her Laura Mercier gloss as she swiveled her head around in search of the production crew. But the Marvils' front foyer was empty.

"How was your day, pickle?" Merri-Lee looped her arm over Dylan's shoulders and led her to the living room, where Jaime and Ryan were chilling on the couches, nibbling on fruit kabobs.

"It was good," Dylan said vaguely. She could count on one hand how many times her family had hung out together in the formal living room. It felt like the set of *The Daily Grind*, only without one wall removed for audience seating.

"Those Citizens are so slimming," Jaime gushed. Dylan turned around to see who she was talking to.

"I'm talking to you, Dylan!" Jaime clarified.

Ryan patted the empty couch cushion next to her. "Come sit. Let's catch up!"

Dylan sat, but not before scouring the room for hidden

cameras. She ran a hand through the chamaedorea palm tree in the corner and then tried to discreetly examine all the decorative pillows. They seemed clear, yet . . . her mother never had time to relax with her daughters on a random afternoon. Her sisters were never this interested in her.

But she couldn't find any evidence of the production team, and her family was looking at her expectantly. So she collapsed onto the couch next to Ryan, released her doubts into a brie-and-raspberry tart, and told them about the clothing sale. They even offered to contribute. An attentive family and delicious foods? A girl could get used to this.

CUT TO:

A little while later, Dylan stood in her walk-in, blaring Ke$ha and pulling items to donate. Out came the old Pradas and Nanette Lepores, the only-worn-once-but-already-way-over-it rompers and miniskirts. As she pruned her closet, she felt like she was shedding another ten pounds.

The unmistakable smell of lasagna drifted past her nose, and Dylan stopped, mesmerized. Merri-Lee's lasagna was a meal legends were made of, but she hadn't made it in at least five years—not since her talk show had taken off and catapulted her into low-carb celebdom.

"Dylly-pie, dinner time!"

Merri-Lee's voice wafted up the stairs and into Dylan's

room, just like the aroma of meat sauce and basil. Her pink Calvin Klein tank fluttered to the floor like a low-fat tortilla, and she dashed out of her room.

"Whoa!" she blurted, running headfirst into the hair and makeup team.

"Touch-up time!" one of the stylists sang.

"Wha—"

But before Dylan could even finish asking what they were doing there, the team quickly rubbed some sticky pomade into her curls, blotted her face, and outlined her eyes and lips. Then there was a final coat of sheer gloss, a straightening of her Marni blouse and jeans, and she was off to claim her dream meal.

In the dining room, Jaime and Ryan, shiny in all the right places and matte everywhere else, sat on either side of Merri-Lee, leaving Dylan to sit at the foot of the table. Not only did the food smell ah-mazing, it looked that way, too. Bowls of crisp garlic bread, hunks of fresh parmesan, and tall pitchers of ice water with lemon wedges surrounded the main event: the lasagna, which sat in the center of the table on Merri-Lee's best crystal serving platter. Dylan sat down and grabbed the Tiffany serving spoon (a gift from the ladies of *The View*), but Ryan kicked her under the table.

"Not yet," she hissed as Walkie-Talkie walked in. He headed straight for Merri-Lee.

"You remember what we talked about, right, Merrily?" He said her name like it was one word and Dylan braced herself. Merri-Lee did nawt like to be mistaken for someone with an adverb as a name. Dylan had learned that lesson even before she knew what an adverb was.

"All set," Merri-Lee muttered through pursed lips. Walkie-Talkie left, the lights went on, and finally Dylan heard the mysterious director yell, "Action!" Without wasting a moment, she cut into the lasagna and began serving herself.

"So, is everyone excited to be back home after our lovely vay-cay?" Merri-Lee asked, squeezing lemon into her water.

Dylan watched Ryan and Jaime for cues on how to respond and then nodded when they did. *How does everyone know what's going on but me?* Dylan assumed that was the price she paid for being late and finger-dragged it to the *oh-well* pile. Technically this was a *reality* TV show, so a little reality every now and then couldn't hurt.

"Jaime-doll, what was it like to see Hunter after all that time apart?"

Hunter Templeton was Jaime's longtime crush. Dylan rolled her eyes. Like Claire in a candy shop, once Jaime got started on the Hunter subject, she couldn't stop.

"It was so sweet," Jaime recalled dreamily. "He met me at the mall and—"

The doorbell interrupted her. Dylan slumped in her seat and waited for the producer to yell "Cut!" but instead, some random maid entered the dining room, followed by a teenager in a Flowers by Algernon polo. He was carrying a massive bouquet of tulips and orchids.

"Ryan Marvil? Flower delivery," he said dully. Everyone looked on in surprise as Ryan accepted the bouquet and opened the card. Everyone, Dylan noticed, except Merri-Lee. Dylan could even swear she caught her mother wink at Walkie-Talkie.

"'Dear Ryan, I saw these flowers and thought of you. Hope you're thinking of me, too. XOXO, Hun—'" Ryan stopped and gaped at Jaime. Jaime leapt up and ripped the card from Ryan's hands.

"Hunter? *My* Hunter sent you flowers?!" She started ripping up the card, sending little white speckles of cardboard across the table.

"Ew, nawt in the lasagna!" Dylan yelled, cupping her hands over her plate.

"I swear, I don't know why he sent these!" Ryan cried. A camera zoomed in and captured the look of anguish on her face.

"Liar! I know he gave you a ride home from Julie's yesterday."

"Yeah, but that was nothing," she said. "He did say I looked good with a tan, but I didn't think—"

"You never do!" Jaime reached out and grabbed the bouquet, spilling green plant food all over the garlic bread. Dylan snagged an unblemished piece before it was ruined, and then froze.

If this had been any other family, she'd have hunkered down with popcorn to watch the fight. But this was *her* family, and something about the whole thing smelled more

suspicious than the combination of Italian food and ferti-
lizer.

Another cameraman ran into the room, taking position
behind Jaime just as she started shrieking and ripping up the
orchids. "I'll never forgive you, Ryan!"

"Loves, can't we figure this out rationally?" Merri-Lee
tried to broker the peace, but Jamie just shrieked again and
Ryan started openly sobbing.

Dylan looked up at Merri-Lee for help. Behind her mother,
she caught sight of the producer low-fiving the cameramen.
The looks of glee on their faces told Dylan all she needed to
know: This whole thing had been a setup. And it would make
great (reality) TV.

"Don't you guys see what's happening here?" Dylan
screeched. Someone had to be the Bruce Jenner in this scene,
and it may as well be her.

"Shut! Up!" Jamie yelled. "You always take her side!"

"Ehma-what?" Dylan said, dumbfounded.

"Girls, let's—" Merri-Lee tried, but not really.

"And *you* always take *her* side!" Ryan screamed. She
stood up and threw her napkin down on the table. "Screw
this. I'm going to go have dinner with Hunter. At least *he*
likes me!"

Jaime looked like she'd been slapped in the face.

The director yelled "Cut!"

So Dylan did. Taking her knife, she sliced into another
piece of lasagna and ate around the petals. For the sake of
"reality."

Merri-Lee opened a cabinet, scanned its contents, and then closed it. She tried the next one, and then the one after that.

"The serving dishes go over here, Mom," Dylan said patiently.

"Silly me! I always forget." Merri-Lee laughed.

Forget? Like you ever knew, Dylan thought—something she was getting used to doing when the cameras were around.

She and her mother were "cleaning up the kitchen" after the disastrous dinner. It was a redundant effort, because production had already cleaned up most of it. But Dylan got the sense that she and "Merrily" were supposed to have some sort of mother-daughter moment. Due to her lack of experience, Dylan recalled the *Gilmore Girls* for inspiration.

"Thanks for helping me clean," Merri-Lee said. She cupped the glass of red wine that production had poured for her and took a seat at the breakfast bar. Once Dylan put away the last of the clean dishes, she joined her and guzzled the Diet Coke that someone had helpfully placed on the counter. *Sponsor much?*

"That was some fight your sisters were having, huh?"

Dylan tensed, feeling the cameraman breathing down her neck as he tried to get his shot. She wondered what he'd do if she took the camera and broke it over his head. Would it be considered good TV?

"Anyway, I'm glad we have this alone time." Merri-Lee's

face was as concerned as her Botox injections would allow. She reached into the pocket of her Vera Wang tunic and held up a small package of pills. The light from the overhead rig reflected off of it, making Dylan squint.

Merri-Lee took a deep breath. "I found these diarrhea pills in your purse."

"*WHAT?*" Dylan gave the producer hovering in the doorway a death stare. "Mom, those are so *nawt* mine."

Merri-Lee put a manicured hand on Dylan's knee. "I'm concerned that you might be taking extreme, unhealthy measures to control your weight. You must face a lot of pressure, having me as a mom. But these"—she waved the packet of pills around—"are not the answer."

The scene was a bigger setup than the latest *Real Housewives* reunion show. *This cannawt be happening*, Dylan thought. She knew those pills had to have been planted by the producer. After all, she had never felt better about her body! The effects of her Caribbean cleanse were still showing, and the shoot schedule had kept her way too busy to sneak extra meals. For the first time, she believed all those celebrities who said they were too busy to eat. Besides, Dylan had enough gas and urgency on a normal day. Why on Earth would she ever want more?

"You have to believe me," she began, staring intently into Merri-Lee's matching green eyes. "Those pills are *not* mine. Someone must have put them in there by mistake. It's okay, though." She patted Merri-Lee's hands. Two could play this game. "I forgive you for accusing me."

Merri-Lee's eyes tightened. "I'm sorry, Dyl-pickle, but I don't believe you. I'm afraid I'm going to have to ground you."

The room fell silent as Dylan felt the repercussions of that word. She was *grounded*? She'd never been grounded in her life. Merri-Lee believed in the Dina Lohan style of parenting—let whatever happens, happen.

Until now, anyway.

Another camera showed up, this time blocking the doorway to the back staircase. Slowly, Dylan slid out of her chair, held her red head up high, and brusquely pushed the camera aside. She stomped up to her room, her Fiorentini & Baker boots echoing in time with the cameraman's rhythm, then slammed the door squarely in his face.

CUT TO:

Lasagna was everywhere. Table after table of steaming, heavenly smelling dishes. She went from one plate to the next, eating a forkful at each station, savoring the perfectly cooked flat noodles, the crushed tomatoes, the cheese . . .

A bright light blinded her. The lasagna was gone. All gone!

Dylan opened her eyes. A bright light was shining in her face. "AHHHHHHHHHHHHHHHHHH!" She shot up in bed and kicked off her covers. But then the light disappeared, and hushed giggles sang out over her bedroom.

Someone whispered, "This scene will be just what we need to claim she's having nightmares about her weight issues!"

The door clicked shut, and Dylan was alone. She collapsed back onto her pillow and yelled into the feathers.

There has to be a way to shut this down, she thought, in case they were still lurking. She tried to think back to Jon Gosselin and his fifteen minutes of fame. How had he managed to get cut from his show?

She stayed awake the rest of the night, watching the moon cross over the sky and realizing for the first time just how much it looked like a giant camera lens.

CUT TO:

When Dylan awoke next, she flailed her arms through the air in case any more cameras were in her face.

She was alone, for now, but the crew was in the house, squeaking around in Converse sneakers and dragging heavy lighting rigs.

Upon catching a glimpse of reflection in the vanity mirror, Dylan nearly fell off her bed. Her normally lush, shiny hair was dull and knotted like Britney's weave. Dark circles that no amount of Clinique All About Eyes could remedy lined her eyes. Her ruby lips had faded to the color of her cheeks, which, thanks to lack of sleep, were Edward Cullen–pale. Her desire to be captured on film today was zero-minus-fifty.

Quietly, she slipped on the closest pair of shoes she could

find. KORS Michael Kors platform clogs didn't complement her flannel pajamas, but only Massie would be thinking about fashion at a time like this. She crept to a window and slowly opened it. The ice-cold wind slapped-and-chapped her on contact.

Crossing one leg over the ledge, she began shimming down. She was making good progress, one step-shimmy-step at a time, when her left clog got caught on the trellis. Without warning, the wood snapped, and just like that, Dylan was headed down, down, down, until she landed—thud!—in the backyard bushes, her clog clinging to life two stories above.

"Ankle," she moaned.

She tried to push herself up to a sitting position but her flannel pajamas were caught in a rosebush. With an impatient tug she forced herself free, leaving an L-for-Loser-shaped piece of fabric dangling from a branch.

"Go! Go!" a voice echoed across the backyard. Suddenly a camera appeared over her, capturing her in her full au naturel glory. Dylan flashed back to all the "Stars without makeup!" features she'd devoured in *Life & Style*. She'd never felt so connected to Heather Locklear before.

The director's voice shouted, "Stay with her. We can make it look like she's sneaking out of the house to escape her mom's punishment! We can position her as the ultimate family rebel—the Khloe to the rest of the family's Kourtney and Kim. Someone who's always been jealous of her sisters and will do anything for attention!"

"Get away!" Dylan screamed as the clog fell from the trellis and bounced off her knee. Pain white-flashed in front of her eyes but she managed to stand and speed-limp toward the garage before the tears came.

But the camera caught every single uneven step.

From the hordes of tracksuit- and sweatpants-clad girls marching through the Riveras' gate, there was no denying that the PC's idea of hosting a hand-me-down clothing swap was going to be a Massie-ive success. Kristen followed the crowd and stumbled up the drive, grateful for Alicia's event-planning ability. It was easy to get lost on the Rivera estate, and even though Kristen had been there dozens of times, it was a maze of marble statues, snow-covered gardens, and unexpected paths that veered off into any number of garages, guesthouses, and sheds.

Luckily, Alicia had thought to order professional, custom signage that marked the way to the backyard tent, where the sale was being held. GREEN IS THE NEW BLACK! shouted the signs, followed by RETHINK YOUR WARDROBE, REUSE OUR CLOTHES in smaller lettering. The grin on Kristen's face grew wider. She wasn't sure if criticizing the LBRs of OCD was the way to get them to spend their money, but from the looks of things, it was working—and not just for OCD, she realized, racing past a group of unfamiliar preteens. Clearly, Alicia's Facebook advertising and promotional Tweets had worked. Students from all over the area, including ADD and even the elementary school, were hand-me-down hungry and anxious to dig in.

Kristen slipped inside the back door of an oversized tent where girls were swarming. Alicia had rented dozens of long tables, clothing racks, and mannequins, and styled the interior like a charming Nolita boutique. Accessories dangled from a piece of chain-link fence, footwear was displayed on columns made of shoeboxes, and barely worn dresses, skirts, jeans, and coats had been divided into sections named after every member of the Pretty Committee and marked with a cardboard cutout of the girl. The Alicia section was crisp and tailored. Kristen's was sporty. Massie's was high-end and eclectic. Dylan's was full of brights and bolds. And Claire's was full of markdowns. The enthusiastic crowd drowned out the Miranda Cosgrove song that was pumping through the speaker system. Amid it all, caterers handed out See's Candies to keep the energy up. Kristen's head throbbed at the overwhelmingness of it all.

Or maybe it was from the brutal practice she'd just endured. Her calves cramped at the memory. She gingerly touched the spot on her arm where Andrea had punched her in delight after she'd scored during a tough drill. Already, it had blossomed into a shiny purple bruise. It was ah-mazing!

A tickle of sweat dripped down her back. "Why is it so *hawt* in here?" she grumbled. She shrugged off her coat, wincing again, and then saw the heat lamps. Alicia had thought of everything!

She stashed her gym bag under the nearest table she

could find. Jennifer's mom had given her a ride to Alicia's, and like she had done so many times before, she changed in the car, swapping her Soccer Sisters gear for a Massie-friendly outfit: skinny black cords, a long-sleeved Elie Tahari tee, and motorcycle boots from DSW. When it came to shedding disguises, she was more qualified than Batman.

"Kristen!" Alicia called.

She slowly raised her arm to wave hello, but when pain radiated up from her bruise, she quickly dropped it and opted for an *I'm-ready-to-help-and-sorry-I'm-late* smile.

But apparently Alicia's smile-decoding skills were off today, because she storm-marched over to Kristen, holding a walkie-talkie up to her ear and another one in her clenched fist.

"PCKG has been spotted in the tent. I repeat, the eagle has landed. Call off the search!" Alicia hiss-commanded into her walkie-talkie. She glared at Kristen. "You're late."

The walkie-talkie cackled to life, carrying Dylan's voice with it. "Who's the eagle again? And why do we care?"

There was another burst of static and Claire's voice wavered over the airwaves. "I thought Massie was the eagle? But she's a dressing room attendant with me."

"Stylist! I'm consulting as the stylist! Gawd, Kuh-laire," Massie's voice corrected.

Alicia rolled her eyes and pressed a button, and the walkie-talkies went dead. "Kristen. Did we or did we *nawt* all iChat last night and agree to be here at one-thirty to help set up?"

"We did," Kristen said, dropping her eyes. She had a perfectly valid excuse for being late. If only she had the courage to share it. "I'm sorry."

"Lucky for you it's all running smoothly—" She paused and pressed a button on the walkie-talkie. "Dylan! Come over to the southwest corner ay-sap!" Then she released it and added, "Unforch, there are still some odd jobs that need to be done. You and Dylan can handle them."

"Whatever you need!" Kristen chirped. Beside her, at least fourteen girls were fighting over a stand-up mirror.

Alicia smoothed her camel-colored Ralph Lauren jacket and eyed Kristen suspiciously. She held out the extra walkie-talkie. "Here. This is yours. We're on channel nine—you know, like Chanel No. 9." She beamed. "My idea."

Dylan arrived, limping over to Kristen and Alicia. As Alicia radioed new directions to Massie and Claire, Kristen studied Dylan's right foot. It was stuffed into a Tory Burch flat, but Kristen could swear it was puffier than normal.

"Hey Leesh," Dylan said. "Did you tell Olivia Ryan that blondes get 10 percent off?"

Alicia rolled her eyes. "Opposite of yes!" She stormed off, but not before shoving the walkie-talkie into Kristen's arm, where it brushed against her bruise. She winced and gripped the area to soothe the pain. She could barely hear as Dylan tried to explain how she and Kristen were tasked with scissor duty.

"Wait, two questions," Kristen interrupted when the blinding pain had abated. "First, what is scissor duty? And second, why are you limping?"

"Third," Dylan corrected her. "Where'd you get that bruise?"

Kristen paused. "Um . . . Beckham. He pounced on me. I seriously need to put him on a diet. Now you answer."

Dylan tossed back her hair. "Scissor duty is the job we're not going to *actually* do, but we'll tell Alicia we did. And I slipped in my new Giuseppe Zanotti heels. There was ice on the driveway."

Alicia's crackled through the walkie-talkie. "Pretty Committee, it's time to regroup. Center table under the chandelier in five. Over."

It took Kristen and Dylan five full minutes to make their way through the crowd to the center table because girls kept pouring into the tent and piling clothes into the reusable shopping bags Alicia had provided. They were five different shades of green, just like the custom signage, and said, REDUCE YOUR CARBON FOOTPRINT. REUSE OUR OLD CLOTHES. RECYCLE THE DESIGNERS WHO MATTER.

Already under the chandelier, Massie waved Kristen and Dylan over to her, Claire, and Alicia.

"It's runway time!" Massie called to them. Her eyes flashed with power. "Alicia had the brilliant idea of having the Pretty Committee show off some of the ah-mazing deals we have today."

Alicia smiled at Massie's praise, but Kristen noticed it didn't quite reach her eyes, which was odd because a compliment from Massie was rarer than a pink diamond.

"I think that's a great idea," Kristen offered.

"I've pulled outfits directly from the racks for each of us. Kuh-laire, for you." Massie presented Claire with a pair of Alicia's wide-legged black pants. On the tag it said: *Purchased from Barneys in November; worn once.* A gauzy floral blouse that matched the blue of Claire's eyes perfectly claimed: *Purchased at Lala in Los Angeles; never worn.*

"Nine point four!" Alicia decided, nodding in approval.

"Kristen, this is for you," Massie declared, handing over a never-before-worn Marc Jacobs romper, paired with Diane von Furstenberg booties whose tag read: *Worn when I met Chace Crawford with my mom on her show; courtesy of Ryan Marvil.*

"Ssshhh." Dylan held a finger to her lips. "I kinda forgot to tell her I was taking this."

"It's perfect," Kristen whispered, running her hands over the smooth romper. It would feel so nice to slip into this and curl up on a couch somewhere. Preferably with some aspirin and an ice pack.

Massie presented the rest of the outfits and then said, "I thought it would be fun to twist things up a bit! So, Alicia, you're wearing Dylan's asymmetric Halston dress from the first week of December—it's a solid nine-eight. And Dylan, you'll be in that Ralph Lauren cape and leather pants Alicia bought during Fashion Week last fall."

"Yesss!" Dylan hissed, grabbing the leather pants. "I've always wanted to be Catwoman!"

"And what about you, Mass?" Alicia asked, gently draping the Halston over her shoulder.

"Moi?" Massie fluttered her eyelashes. "I'm modeling Alicia's Tibi ankle pants and Dylan's Alice + Olivia sequin tee. Something from each of you!" She held up the items and the girls gasped.

"Ten! Ten!" they all agreed.

"This is incredible!" Claire exclaimed, unwrapping a fresh pack of SweeTarts and bouncing on her toes.

"People must be freaking out over everything here," Kristen added, surveying the masses.

All around them, girls were snatching up jackets and blouses and belts with faster hands than Winona Ryder in a department store. Everyone had at least two full bags. "It's all so ah-mazing. And ah-ffordable!" She glanced at the price tag Alicia had hand-written into the romper. It was almost as cheap as the most expensive sweater she'd ever bought at H&M!

"Group hug!" Dylan shouted, and the PC crowded in together for a big squeeze. Kristen tried not to wince again.

"Okay, time's up. We have a schedule to stick to!" Alicia clapped her hands twice.

"Sorry," Dylan mumbled as her phone vibrated. "I have to take this." She started punching into her keyboard.

"Let's get suited up and start the runway show," Alicia added.

Dylan's phone buzzed again.

"Who is that?" Kristen asked. "All of your friends are here."

"Mmm-hmm," she nodded, thumbing away.

"So let's go," Alicia urged, pulling on Dylan's arm.

"Two secs," Dylan muttered. Her cheeks were slowly turning the color of her hair, and Kristen could see she was biting her lip. Her eyes kept bouncing back and forth between the walkie-talkie she'd been assigned and her Evo, like she couldn't decide which piece of technology needed her more.

"Oh, I know why you're stalling," Massie said assuredly. She clucked her tongue. "Don't worry, Dyl. Alicia's old leather pants will *toe*-dally fit you. I made sure of it!"

"That's not it," Dylan mumbled.

"*Ehma*-workload! You're just trying to get out of the rest of the sale duties!" Alicia challenged. "Well, forget it. We all have to help out. Even if *some* of us would rather be elsewhere!"

Kristen reddened. She could swear Alicia's eyes were boring a hole directly through her tee and into her bruise.

"I promise, that's not it," Dylan begged. Her phone jingled again.

"Fine," Alicia huffed. She snapped her fingers twice. "Change of plans! If Dylan's too busy to take the runway right now, she can go handle the registers."

"Tiny Nathan needs a break, anyway," Claire offered. "He and Todd have been complaining about child labor violations."

"Kristen, since you were late, you can go help Dylan with the register," Alicia commanded. Her walkie-talkie burst to life in her hands.

A voice that sounded suspiciously like Layne's rang out over the headset. "Alicia, we've got a style infraction in the dressing rooms. Over."

Alicia grabbed Massie's arm like it was the last pair of Rag & Bone gloves in Westchester. "Uh oh. Someone must be having a *What Not to Wear* moment. I need you! Girls, runway is happening in thirty minutes. No excuses!"

Dylan's phone rang again, and Alicia glared at her one last time before pulling Massie and Claire along with her. Kristen sighed and followed Dylan to their next task.

The runway show had been a total success, and Kristen and Dylan were back at the registers as Kristen, the math whiz, tried desperately to remember how to subtract someone's fifty-seven-dollar purchase from the one-hundred-dollar bill she'd been handed.

"Excuse me, ma'am, but I should get forty-three dollars back, not twenty," complained the girl.

"Ma'am!" Dylan burped.

"What? *Ehma*-I'm-so-sorry," Kristen said, turning purple and quickly handing the girl the rest of her change. Maybe it was the lack of food, or the temperature inside the heated tent, or the leftover nerves from the catwalk, but Kristen was suddenly feeling like she'd just ridden a roller coaster three times in a row. A feeling she hadn't had since she was eight . . . when she rode a roller coaster three times in a row.

"You messed up my change, too," the girl's friend said. They were the last two customers in line, and Kristen was so woozy that she couldn't be sure if there were actually two of them, or if she was seeing double.

Dylan pulled out money from her own pocket and handed it to the girl. "Thanks for being green and buying our old clothes. Now scram!"

Kristen was about to thank Dylan for saving her when Alicia's voice screeched through their walkie-talkies. "Dylan! Kristen! I heard that! If you can't figure out how to make change, you may as well just give up now."

"Spare us your lecture," Dylan hissed into the walkie-talkie. "You're gonna be thrilled when you hear the day's totals!"

Alicia, Massie, and Claire came running over to the registers. Everyone held their breath as Kristen finished counting out the small stacks of bills that lined the now-empty table. Then she handed it to Dylan to recount it, just in case she was SSD: still seeing double.

"Two thousand eight hundred and fifty-three dollars!" she announced. Massie's eyes welled up and her face blanched like she'd just seen the ghost of Christmas past—and it was carrying presents.

"Ah-mazing!" Alicia clapped.

"Great job, Alicia. Great job, everyone!" Kristen slurred.

Dylan gave her a questioning look, but thankfully no one else noticed.

But if she kept up this double life for much longer, eventually they would.

"Killer sequins, Massie!"

"Best recycling sale ever!"

"You were born to be on the runway!"

As Massie waved good-bye to New Isaac, she practically skipped up the steps to her front door as she remembered the compliments her public had heaped on her back at Alicia's. It was more official than Miley and Liam's breakup: The day had been a total success. And perhaps more important, everyone at OCD and the surrounding schools were sure to be talking about Massie's ah-mazingly styled outfits for weeks to come. Dozens of seventh graders would return after break with sequins on their old Gap tees just so they could look like Massie had on the runway, glittering and sparkling. She couldn't wait to text Landon the news.

All of the anxiety she'd been feeling about whether her financial status would affect her alpha status was gone. If today proved anything—apart from her inevitable career as the next Anna Wintour—it was that her friends and class-mates still ah-dored her.

With a new spring in her step, Massie opened the front door, pulled off her Dior sunglasses, and greeted Bean with a humongous kiss on the forehead.

She smiled at her reflection in the foyer mirror, and for the first time in weeks it smiled back. Her amber eyes were vibrant and perfectly contoured from her Stila Jewel eyeshadow palette, and her hair was tousled just the right amount. So what if she had to sell old clothes to raise money? She *looked* rich. And, thanks to her ah-mazing friends, she felt rich. Massie wouldn't ever forget the way the PC kept her secret and rallied around her today. It was like having her own personal glee club, without all the ah-nnoying singing.

"Ehmagawd," she said to the mirror. "Those poor people were right!"

"Massie, is that you?" Kendra's voice sang out from the kitchen.

Massie followed the scent of scorched chocolate. It smelled like someone had tried—and failed—to bake brownies. Massie pulled open the sleek trash drawer beside the sink. Sure enough, an upside-down charred cake had been dumped on top. It closed with a bang. Why did her parents insist on playing *Top Chef* when Inez wasn't around? They inevitably turned the place into *Hell's Kitchen*, without the kitchen. But like her, they were trying their best. Stopping at nothing to survive. Because that's what alphas do. No matter what. It was in their blood.

"I've been saving some money," Massie said, channeling the stack of hundreds in her wallet. "Let's go to the bakery and load up. You drive, I buy."

Hearing the words come from her mouth warmed Massie

more than an open oven ever could. After all these years of taking from her parents she was finally in the position to give back. It bolstered her self-worth in a way that all the black diamonds at Barneys couldn't. If she had to be the breadwinner, so be it. As long as the word *winner* was involved, she was on board.

"Come sit with us." William pulled out the bar stool in between him and Kendra.

They were seated at the breakfast bar, their mouths set in grim, straight lines. Massie's stomach tightened and her good mood deflated faster than a punctured yoga ball. Her parents suddenly looked very, very tired.

"Is everything okay?" Massie asked, her speeding heart already seeming to know.

Kendra took Massie's hands in hers. If felt like being stuck in the ice cube maker.

"We know things have been really tough around here," William said, smoothing the imaginary hair on his bald head. "So as a token of our gratitude, we have something for you."

Space heaters? Take-out? High-speed Internet?

Massie glanced back and forth between her parents. She didn't know what to expect.

Kendra slid a rectangular, black Barneys box across the counter and into Massie's hands. But she refused to get excited. The boxes could be bought on eBay for under five dollars. For all she knew they'd put a key inside for some brand-new bike lock. The bike, which was probably on layaway, would be all hers by senior prom.

"Open it," William urged.

Massie managed to smile as she lifted the lid. "*What? You're kidding, right?*"

Inside was the black diamond bracelet, the one she'd dreamed of hugging her wrist for weeks, and the matching black diamond earrings. It was a post-Christmas miracle!

She snapped the lid shut. "Be honest. Did you do anything illegal to get this?"

"No, silly!" Kendra pulled Massie into a squishy hug while William laughed loudly.

"I got a new job!" her dad added. Bean barked.

Kendra clapped. "We're in the black."

"More like the green!" William said, high-fiving his wife.

The world spun as Massie tried to process the news—and the fact that her parents seemed to high-five now. She had just made poor cool, and rich was already back? She couldn't just spring this on the LBRs. Not after today. They trusted her when she told them used clothes would be huge next semester. If she switched back to retail before spring, they'd revolt. Trends took time to turn. It's the cycle of life, even at Target. You can't stock the shelves with skinny jeans one day and boot cut the next. It's confusing, even to the LBRs.

"Massie?"

"Are you okay?"

She heard her parents speaking but couldn't respond. Echoes of their earlier words still reverberated in her head. *New job . . . in the green . . . black diamonds . . .*

"*Ehmagawd!*" Massie cried, springing up from her stool as she realized exactly what the words meant. Who cared about the LBRs? The only thing that mattered was that there was life after death! Like a beautiful butterfly emerging from a cold cocoon, she would live to fly again. She hugged her mom and swung her around in a circle. "We're rich again!" Bean yipped excitedly and started licking William's toes. This was the best news she'd ever heard, including the time Landon told her she had the most kissable lips he'd ever seen. By the time he returned from Bali, everything would be back to normal. He'd never have to know how close she had come to financial ruin.

"Is Inez coming back? What about Isaac? And the heat, can we turn it on now? Can I go shopping? No, maybe I'll move my stuff back from Claire's. I was thinking of painting my room green. Not a forest green or a kelly, more like a spring green. Something fresh and new. But I desperately need a manicure! Mom, let's go together. Dad, you come, too. Then we'll go for sushi and—"

"There's more," William said.

Massie bounced on her toes in anticipation. "Tell me, tell me, tell me!" *A trip to Belize? Cabo? Bali to meet Landon?*

"Well," William said, disentangling himself from Massie. "We're still moving . . ."

Huh?

"But to an even bigger house. In fact, it's a castle!"

Massie gasped so hard she got an ice cream headache. Her Sweet Sixteen would be royal! She always knew she was meant to live like a queen. "Wait, not White Castle, right?" she asked, suddenly in the mood for jokes.

Kendra and William exchanged a look. Massie's stomach dipped. "What? You didn't buy a White Castle franchise, did you? Because I was kidding and that would not be okay and—"

"No." William managed a smile. "This is a real castle."

Massie sat back on the stool. Her weakening knees warned her that it might be a good idea. Or was that her internal compass, telling her that there weren't any castles in Westchester? "Where is it?" she dared.

"Just across the pond," her father said.

"That brown duck pond?" Massie furrowed her brow, picturing the swampy pool that separated Westchester from the next county over. "Oh. I suppose that would be okay . . . maybe we can turn it into a natural hot spring. And with Isaac back I—"

"No, Massie," Kendra said quietly.

"'The Pond' is a nickname for the Atlantic," William said.

"*Ocean?*"

Her parents nodded.

"We're moving to England," Kendra whispered.

Massie jumped to her feet. "The European England?" Suddenly her knees felt more wobbly than Claire in heels. Her breath coming in shallow rasps. Besides the princes— one of whom was already spoken for—what was waiting for her in England? Some Harry Potter school? Fish sticks?

More soccer? Excuse me, *football*. What about OCD? The Pretty Committee? Landon? High school? Brownie? Galwaugh Farms? The mall? "Can't you commute?"

"To London?" William scoffed.

"England isn't so different from Westchester," Kendra tried.

"Except it's completely different!" Massie tried to swallow, but her throat refused to cooperate. Her whole body felt just like the brownies her parents had tried to bake: over and done.

"You'll be going to a wonderful private school," William continued, trying to sound encouraging. "And my office is right down the street from our castle, so I'll be able to spend more time at home."

William started to tell her more about life in England, but his lips looked like they were moving in slow motion. Massie put her hand on the kitchen counter to brace herself, but it seemed to shrink and move out of the way.

She thought her father started to say something about changing their last name from Block to Bloke, but she couldn't focus.

"Am I London Bridge?" she mumbled.

Kendra held her ice-cold hand up to Massie's forehead. "Are you okay?"

"Then why am I falling down?"

Just like her father's financial statement, Massie was in the black.

CURRENT STATE OF THE UNION

IN	OUT
Sale-ing for New Year's	Sailing for New Year's
American Apparel	American Express
The Simple Life	The Life

"Layne, we told you. We're not wearing those," Harris said, tapping his drumstick with every syllable.

"No way, no how," Derrington added.

"What's wrong with them?" Layne asked incredulously. She pointed to Claire. "You like them, right?"

Claire surveyed Layne's outfit. It had been hard not to notice it when she arrived at the Fishers' garage for another band practice, but it was only now, under the bright lights that Cam had set up to make the garage seem more stadium-like, that she could see the intricacies that made it, as Massie would say, *Layme*. A silver-and-blue unitard with gloves ran the length of her arms with a matching headband. She'd painted silver streaks on her cheekbones and was sporting silver lipstick. *Avatar-u serious?*

"Well," Claire started to say. "I think they're really orig—" But her eyes quickly moved to Cam, who was making a "cut it out" sign with his hands. "They're . . . well, you know me, Layne. I still wear flared jeans, so what do I know?"

"I just don't understand why you guys insist on wearing regular street clothes," Layne protested. Her breath echoed into the microphone as she glared at the band. "We have Lady Gaga and Katy Perry to compete with!"

"Who?" Derrington asked.

Claire giggled.

"No costumes," Harris said. "And that's final."

"Boys!" Mrs. Fisher opened the door that led to the house. She was pretty for a mom, with dark brown hair, green eyes, and a warm smile. It was obvious where the boys got their looks. "Come say goodbye to your grandparents."

Harris stood up from his drum set.

"Be right back," Cam said to Claire. "Grandma always sneaks me a twenty when Mom's not looking."

"Anyone want some chips?" Derrington asked, trailing behind them.

Claire shook her head no, grateful for the alone time with Layne.

"I seriously can't believe we're going to be neighbors." Layne said, joining Claire on the old brown corduroy couch facing the band. "I rewired my walkie-talkies so your house is in range and clocked the bike ride between our places. Nineteen seconds if you take the left side and sixteen if you take the right. The curve near the Adelmans' adds time but the sidewalk on that side has fewer nicks so it's kind of a win-win." She dug out a Slim Jim from somewhere within the depths of her costume and began chewing loudly. Claire swapped her one for a Swedish Fish, and they munched, happily imagining the possibilities.

"We should make sure to have copies of each other's house keys, too," Layne continued. Bursts of crumbs flew out of her mouth and landed on the unitard, smearing orange powder over the stretchy silver fabric. "That way we can borrow each other's clothes all the time. And we can probably build some sort of secret underground passage from my bedroom window to yours. We can smuggle homework answers back and forth!"

Claire tried to picture borrowing from Layne's closet. She couldn't imagine what Massie would say if she showed up at OCD in silver spandex. She shook her head to clear the image.

"What's wrong?"

Tears gathered behind Claire's eyes. "I'm so excited to be your neighbor and to have our own house," she started. "But . . . what if moving off the Block estate means I'm moving out of the Pretty Committee? What if I was only there because Kendra forced Massie to let me in?"

"What did Massie say when you told her?" Layne asked, seeming as normal as one could in an avatar costume.

Claire sighed, too embarrassed to admit she hadn't found the courage to tell the alpha yet.

Layne, like the best friend she was, guessed it anyway. "She doesn't *know*?"

Silence. The question hung in the air like Todd's cologne.

Finally, Layne gripped Claire by the shoulders. "Do you seriously think that girl would be your friend because Mommy made her? Did you block out your first few months in Westchester? The ones where her mother wanted her to include you? The ones where she threw smoked salmon at your body?" She giggled.

"What?" Claire asked, not finding the memory particularity funny. In fact it brought back full body pains that could have passed for tetanus. "Why are you laughing?"

"I said, 'block out.' Get it? Pretty clever, right?"

Despite her anguish, Claire couldn't help smiling. Her phone buzzed with an incoming text.

Massie: Where r u?
Claire: Cam's. What's up?

Minutes later a loud horn sounded outside and honked until Claire pulled up the creaky garage door. Glaring headlights from a limousine aimed directly at her.

"Kuh-laire!" called Massie, waving from the open moon roof. "Ditch the avatar and get in!"

Her head disappeared and Claire looked at Layne, who rolled her eyes. "Maybe now's a good time to tell her about the house. It seems like she's in a good mood—better hurry before the wind shifts."

"I can't just run out like that," Claire said, even though she was dying to know where the limo came from. Because if she used the sale money for—

The horn honked again.

"Practice is probably over anyway," Layne offered. "I'll tell Cam you had to run."

That was all the encouragement Claire needed. She high-fived Layne and ran down the driveway. The door opened from the inside as she approached.

"Claiiiiirrreeee," Dylan burped in greeting, her red hair catching the moonlight.

"Come in, come in!" Kristen squealed, pulling Claire's arm. She climbed inside and settled between Alicia and Dylan.

"Please don't tell me you wasted all our money on *this*," Claire said.

Ignoring the question, Massie passed her a champagne glass filled with sparkling pomegranate juice. As her arm brushed past Claire, an unfamiliar bracelet caught the light and twinkled like a constellation. She blinked in awe.

"Massie, are you a ski resort?" Claire asked.

"No," the alpha said, raising an eyebrow in a *this-better-be-good* sort of way.

"Then what's with all the black diamonds?"

Everyone burst out laughing, even Massie. Claire's teeth chattered with joy. Then she turned to Alicia. "What are we doing here?" she whisper-asked.

"Gawd," Alicia snapped. "Just because I ran point on the sale doesn't mean I'm in charge!"

Claire held up her hands. "Sorry. Just asking."

"Attention," Massie called, tapping her lip gloss onto the side of her champagne glass so it chimed. "This is an emergency GLU meeting."

Claire's stomach dropped. Had Massie found out about Claire's new house—and that Claire hadn't told her? Or was it something even worse? She glanced around. Dylan was chewing on her hair and then spitting it out, looking disgusted at the taste of it. Alicia was bouncing her left leg up and down so fast, it was like she was inventing a new dance routine. And Kristen was retying her ponytail again and again. They all stared at Massie with wide, guarded eyes. Claire didn't have to borrow Alicia's sterling monogrammed Chanel compact to know that she probably looked just as concerned as the rest of them.

And then Massie broke into an earring-to-earring grin. "So," she began, "I was thinking of changing my name to nachos."

"Why?" Alicia asked for the rest of them.

"Because I'm fully loaded!" she roared, her eyes lit up like a Christmas tree—the ones Sven decorated, not the sad, pathetic one from this year.

Claire's jaw dropped. Alicia's leg stopped moving. Dylan's hair settled around her face. Kristen's ponytail hung limply. The only sound was of the limousine's tires skating along the icy roads outside.

"I'm rich again!" Massie explained to their blank faces.

And then a thunderstorm of cheers rang out. The limo driver shut the partition while the girls squealed with delight. Claire was practically rendered deaf when Alicia screamed, "You're still the alpha!"

Dylan raised her sparkling juice for a toast to congratulate Massie, and everyone quickly joined in. Claire tried to smile, too, but she found it harder than lying to Layne about her costumes for the band. Swedish Fish sloshed around in her stomach, and the sharp turns the limo driver was making weren't helping. Because if the Blocks were rich again, it meant they probably weren't moving.

Which meant she needed to tell Massie the Lyonses *were*. Ay-sap.

Massie watched as Dylan shut the limousine door and then waved goodbye as she limped up the driveway to the Marvils' house. Now that everyone had been dropped off, Massie dropped her smile and allowed the muscles in her face to take five. The audience had gone. She could stop performing. Of course Claire was still there, but she didn't count.

As the familiar streets of Westchester rolled by, Massie tried to imagine London. Would her new neighborhood be cobbled and dusty, with flower sellers trolling for tuppence? Would their castle have a moat to distance them from the masses? Would the clip-clop of horse hooves make her long for Brownie? Would she ever eat sushi with her best friends again?

Massie tried to keep her glossed lip from quivering as she replayed the scene in the limo. How could she possibly tell the Pretty Committee she was leaving? Their relationship was symbiotic. She was their hero; they gave her life meaning. They were the planets; she was their sun. They revolved around her; she brightened their world. Without her they'd be as dark as Seattle; without them she'd just be plain old hot.

When they passed OCD, Claire's voice cut through the silence. "So, tell me what's really going on."

Massie turned away from the window. Was she that transparent? Or did Claire know her too well?

Claire was staring at her with a look of open concern, wearing one of her *I'm-here-for-a-heart-to-heart* expressions. The pane that divided the backseat from the driver was already up but Massie pressed it again, just in case it had failed to make a complete seal.

Claire's voice grew hushed. "Are your money problems really over or did you use the sale money to rent this limo?"

"Puh-lease, I would never do that!" she snapped, genuinely insulted. "I wasn't lying. My dad got a new job. And he'll be making ah-lot." She hesitated. "But you know how it goes. Mo' money, mo' problems."

"Um, not really," Claire smiled, to show she wasn't offended.

Massie sighed. Maybe telling Claire would feel like a Dylan-burp after a big meal.

"We're moving," she began, sampling the taste of truth on her tongue.

"Really?" Claire beamed.

"Don't look too upset," Massie hissed.

"No, it's just that I've been meaning to tell you something all week and this kind of makes it easier."

Massie hiccupped. Other than a sneeze here or there it was the first time Claire ever heard her body betray her. "What?" she asked wearily, like one more surprise and she'd stroke out.

"My parents bought a house. It's right near Layne's,"

Claire broke the news gently. "We're moving, too . . . Ohmigod, where are you going? Maybe we'll be neighbors!" She lowered her blue eyes. "You know, if you still want to hang out and stuff."

"Why?" Massie practically spat. "Now that we're not sharing a house you don't want to be friends?"

"No!" Claire insisted. "I was scared you wouldn't want to be my friend anymore."

Massie would have been flattered if she hadn't been so annoyed. Of course she wanted to stay friends. Why was that even a question? And more importantly, wasn't this about *Massie's* move?

"Kuh-laire, are you a female sheep?"

"No."

"Then why are we even talking about ewe?"

"So that's it?" Claire asked. "I'm still in the Pretty Committee?"

"Depends."

Claire bit her thumbnail. "On what?"

"On whether there *is* a Pretty Committee."

"What?"

"My dad's job isn't in Westchester, Kuh-laire. It's far."

Claire considered this. "Far like Manhattan? Or far like . . . California?"

"Across the pond, far."

"*New Jersey?*" She looked horrified. Massie had taught Claire enough in the past year to know that Jersey and Massie went together like fro-yo and OJ.

A strangled sob escaped from Massie and she felt a tear slip through her Givenchy-ed lashes. "We're moving to some castle . . . in England." Her black diamond bracelet glinted in the moonlight. It felt like a handcuff, binding her to a future of uniform schools and a Madonna accent.

Claire's blue eyes widened in horror. "But England is another *country*!"

Massie nodded in despair. Suddenly, her lone tear had friends and they were riding her cheekbones like kids at a water park.

"But you can't leave," Claire added, her voice cracking like Justin Bieber's.

"Oh really? What am I supposed to do?" Massie's tears fell harder. "Move in with you?"

For a few moments, the only sounds in the limousine were sniffles.

"Why not? You could spend a month with each of us," Claire said suddenly, wiping away her tears. "At least until the end of the semester." Her voice grew excited. "Maybe by then your dad will have a new job here and move back."

As Massie considered this, the weight on her A-cups started to lift. Stay in Westchester? Continue to be the PC's alpha? Invite Landon to the eighth-grade prom? Remain within driving distance of the Westchester Mall and Fifth Avenue? Her Visa-signing hand tingled with possibility. Maybe Claire was onto something. Surely Kendra and William would be willing to let her finish out the year at OCD—and surely the Riveras, Lyonses, Gregorys, and Marvils would love to have her as a guest. Who wouldn't?

But Massie wasn't one for house-surfing like some per-snickety exchange student. She'd much prefer to find one home and hunker down. It was best for everyone: clothes and dog included. But whose? There were pluses and minuses to each.

ROOMMATE	PLUS	MINUS
Dylan	Big house Good wardrobe Cool mom	A lot of girls in one house. Could be alpha struggles.
Alicia	Big house Good wardrobe Nice parents	Alicia is always at dance practice. Will it be creepy hanging alone at her house all the time?
Kristen	Tons of help with homework	Apartment Cat Strict mom
Claire	Feels most like home	Todd Layne Junk food

All things considered, they say you never truly know someone until you live with them. And so it was settled. Goldilocks-ing would begin tomorrow.

Turning onto her street, the view outside the window no longer seemed melancholy. Massie didn't have to burn each passing tree, house, and mailbox into her memory. Her thoughts were free to wander; eyes free to glaze. Massie could take Westchester, and all that comes with it, for granted just like she always had.

And always would.

"First stop: Dylan's." Massie scooped up her pug in her left arm and pulled up the handle on her traveling Louis. "Great wardrobe, cool mom, spacious." The wheels of her Louis roller crunched over what remained of the snow as she pulled her essentials up the driveway to the A-framed house.

In the still light of the afternoon, Dylan's house loomed over Massie, casting a long V-shaped shadow over her and Bean. She fished through her Kooba bag until her freshly manicured hands brushed against the cold Tiffany's key ring. One of the smartest things she'd ever done was insist on a house key from every member of the PC in case she ever wanted to throw them a surprise party. But this was just as good. She couldn't wait to pop in on the Marvils. And couldn't imagine that they would mind. If they did, it was a huge red flag. And she would gladly take the pleasure of her company elsewhere.

Slowly, she turned the key and pushed in the door, stepping slyly into the foyer. Mission Goldilocks was officially underway!

"Sshhh," Massie whispered to Bean as she dragged her Louis in behind her. She pushed her new Prada sunglasses on top of her head and blinked, letting her eyes adjust to the dimmer lights.

As they did, they landed on something unusual. Lining the back wall of the foyer, just under the grand staircase, was a row of television cameras, lighting rigs, director's chairs, and equipment. Was Merri-Lee doing a special filming of her show at home? Or maybe she was planning on broadcasting live from her famous New Year's Yves party, which she was hosting at her house this year?

"Hullo?" she called.

"Massie?" Dylan's shocked voice cut across the stillness of the foyer. She poked her head out from the study and urgently waved Massie inside.

Gently, she closed the door behind them and whispered, "What are you doing here?"

Dylan's hair was styled in perfect ringlets that only a professional could do, and her makeup expertly accented her shining eyes and high cheekbones. She was wearing a Stride gum–pink cashmere sweater dress and thigh-high gray boots.

"Why do you look so ah-mazing?" Massie asked.

"Ssshhhh!" Dylan hissed, covering Massie's mouth. Massie puckered up her glossed lips and Dylan snapped her hand back, frowning at the cranberry-colored stain now outlined on the palm of her hand.

"What's the big deal?" Massie's voice trailed off as she surveyed the study. Dylan often hosted PC fashion shows and movie nights in this very room, so it wasn't like Massie was some sort of stranger to it. But today, it looked like a completely different space. The big leather chairs that faced the granite fireplace had been pushed to the side wall, and the matching leather couch was littered with stacks of papers and laptops. Two cameras were perched on tripods on the far side of the room, and oversized spotlights, turned off, brushed against the tall ceiling.

Dylan's cheeks grew two spots of red as Massie registered what was going on. Cameras . . . scripts . . . Dylan's flawless wardrobe and makeup . . . the constant texts . . . the unexplained absences . . . Massie was no mathematician, but it all added up perfectly.

"*Ehmagawd*, I so smell what you're cooking!" Massie exclaimed. "Are you shooting a reali—"

"Shhhh! You have to hide—now!" Dylan said in a panicked voice, steering Massie toward the powder room off the study.

"Wait! I have something to tell you, too," Massie insisted, digging her wedge heels into the cobalt blue cowhide rug. She took a deep breath. "The reason we're rich again . . ."

" . . . is because your dad got a new job," Dylan nodded. "Yeah, yeah. You told me that. Now go—"

"Right. But what I didn't tell you is that the new job is . . . *nawt* in Westchester." Massie bit her lip as Dylan's face registered the news. "It's nawt even in the United States. Dylan . . . It's in England."

Dylan's face blanched. "England?"

Massie nodded.

"How long have you known this? Why didn't you tell me? When are you leaving? Are you sure?" Her eyelashes buckled under the weight of her tears.

"Cut!" a loud voice called from behind the palm tree in the corner. Massie jumped. Then she noticed the small microphone clipped to Dylan's bib necklace.

"Dylan, try that again. One question at a time."

"Ehmagawd!" Massie snapped.

"Wait a minute," Dylan brightened. She faced the palm. "Did you put her up to this?" And then to Massie, "Are you really moving to England or did they make you say that?"

Massie touched her friend's shoulder. "This really is a reality show? D, how long has this been going on?"

Dylan hung her head. "I'msosorryifIdidn'tkeepthisasecret theywouldhaveputmeinjailit'sbeensohardpleasedon'tbemadat me!"

"It's okay. I get it. You had no choice."

Dylan nodded bravely.

"Before we go again," said the voice behind the palm. "I'd love to see some tears from May-see. Remember, you're leaving."

"You got that right," Massie snapped, scooping up Bean. Her reality was dramatic enough. The last thing she needed was a talking palm tree making it worse.

"Massie, wait! I am so sorry! I had no idea they were filming this!" Dylan eyes were desperate and unhinged. "Are you leaving my house or leaving Westchester? Was the England thing true?"

Massie nodded sadly.

A thin man with a belt full of walkie-talkies appeared before Massie and Bean. "I'm gonna need you to sign this."

"What is it?"

"A confidentiality agreement."

"I'm not eighteen," Massie fired back.

He squinted his beady brown eyes. "Then have your parents sign it."

Massie squinted back. "I don't think they'll appreciate knowing you filmed me without my consent."

"It's legal in New York State."

"With *minors*?"

The guy began flipping through the contract. Bean growled.

"I didn't think so."

Massie turned back and wiggled her thumbs at Dylan, letting her know she'd text later.

"Wait, where are you going?" Dylan called, desperately. The cameras began to roll again.

"To tell everyone your secret," Massie smiled.

"No, Massie, you can't!"

"Correction, Dyl, *you* can't," she said as she pushed past the thin man, "but I can."

From the middle of the cobalt cowhide, Dylan blew Massie a *what-would-I-do-without-you* kiss, her tear-soaked face lighting up like a sun shower.

When Massie reached the Riveras' front door, her arm ached from dragging her Louis luggage up yet another long driveway. The elderly gentleman—Old New Isaac—who was now driving the Range Rover seemed way too frail to help. The last thing Massie needed was for him to wipe out on the ice and break a hip. It had been hard enough finding this one during the holidays.

The sun was setting, and the white twinkle lights that lined the walkway had just flickered on. Massie flipped through her Tiffany keychain until she came to Alicia's key.

"*Hola*," Massie called when she opened the front door. "Anyone home?"

Aside from the strobing Christmas tree in the living room, the house was dark.

"Come on, Bean," she said, setting the pug down on the floor and watching her sniff her new surroundings. She looked ah-dorable in her latest purchase from Bark Jacobs—a fur-trimmed cashmere doggie vest.

The padding of feet echoed throughout the cavernous rooms and Massie froze. Bean barked. But it was just Jenni, the Riveras' Swedish au pair.

"Massie, you scared me. Alicia is practicing," she

explained, pointing the way to the dance studio Alicia's parents had put in for her the summer before. As if Massie needed directions.

Bean trotted along as Massie wound her way through the art-filled hallways. As she stepped into the courtyard, she heard a loud tapping. Massie paused to look up at the sky. "Sounds like hail!"

Bean started whimpering. "Ssshhh," Massie cooed, but her heart started beating faster, too. The dark yard seemed darker and more filled with shadows than it ever had before. Since when had the Riveras' house become a scene in *Scream*?

"Eeeeee!" Massie screeched as she and Bean ran toward the studio. "Leesh! Help!" she called as pushed open the door. Once inside the sound of a thousand pennies falling on a tin roof blared louder than neon lights.

Massie gasped. Alicia's dance troupe was tapping. *Clickety-clack-tap* went their high-heeled tap shoes on the tiles, making a thunderstorm of noise that hit Massie and Bean like a tidal wave. In their plain black leotards with their hair slicked back into high ponytails, Alicia's troupe looked like a remake of Beyoncé's "Single Ladies" video.

Massie watched in awe as Alicia spun and twirled, kicked and posed. When the song finally stopped, Bean wheezed and shook like she'd just found out her new doggie sweater was made of faux fur.

"Let's take five!" Alicia called. The girls made a mad dash for their SmartWaters. "What are you doing here?"

"Surprise," Massie said weakly.

"What's going on? Why do you have luggage?" Alicia panted, her C-cups rising and falling like an ocean buoy. Massie could feel the eyes of the six other girls boring into her, so she grabbed Alicia and pulled her into the hallway just outside the studio. "Remember how I told you that we're rich again?"

Alicia lifted her arm to wipe a trickle of sweat that threatened to drip off the tip of her nose. "Given!"

"Well . . ." *Why was this so hard?* Shouldn't it be getting easier each time she did it—like lip-kissing? Or math? "Listen, here's the thing. We're rich again because my dad got a new job. Only the job isn't in Westchester. It's . . ."

"Ehmagawd, Manhattan!" Alicia nodded wisely. "It's okay, Massie. My dad's in Manhattan half the week for work. You'll get used to seeing him less often." She reached out her toned arms to hug Massie.

Massie shrugged out of Alicia's humid embrace. "His new job isn't in Manhattan, Leesh. It's in England. The country."

Massie waited a beat while Alicia's face registered the news. Her face paled and her Fresh Sugar–glossed lips seemed to lose some of their shimmer.

"And you're going?" Alicia whispered.

"Eventually." Massie's stomach lurched, unwilling to accept the news.

Suddenly Alicia's brown eyes widened in horror. She had never seen her beta look so scared. Not even when Massie told her last April Fool's Day that OCD was enacting a strict "No Ralph Lauren" dress code.

"*Hermia!*" she growled, like the name was a curse.

"Hermia? What's *she* got to do with this?" Massie asked, perplexed.

Alicia sighed and held up her phone. "Hermia was running a special last week. So I got another reading from her. And Massie . . ." Alicia sniffled as her eyes grew bright. "She told me I'd need to become a leader soon. But I don't *want* to be the alpha! You're the only alpha the PC can have!"

"Well, ah-bviously. But that's why I'm here. I'm testing everyone's houses to see if I could move in and finish out the year at OCD. Can I sleep over tonight?"

Alicia's shoulders sagged in obvious relief. "Given times ten! Pick any guest room you want."

Feelings of hope zipped up Massie's spine.

Behind them, the tap troupe was lining up for round two. "I better go." Alicia said. "Make yourself comfortable. My parents should be home soon."

"How much longer do you have to practice?" Massie wondered. Not that Alicia's parents weren't nice. They were. But they were hardly *curl-up-on-the-couch-and-watch*-DWTS material.

"Another hour and a half," Alicia said, stretching her hamstrings. "After that we can hang."

"*Why?* Is today special or something?"

"We practice every day for three hours," Alicia explained.

"We're trying to get into the competitive circuit. But once school starts again, we'll probably cut it down to just one hour a day." Her eyes lit up like two idea light bulbs. "Hey! Why don't you join my tap class? You'll be here all the time anyway."

Just then an Enrique Iglesias song blared through the studio.

"Maybe . . ." *If I fall down a flight of stairs, suffer extreme memory loss, and you somehow manage to convince me that before the accident I thought this was cool.*

"Yay." Alicia smiled and waved as she *click-clacked* off to join the troupe.

Louis, Bean, and Massie returned to the main house. It was still quiet and dark. Long shadows made Bean cower behind Massie. She whimpered when they passed the tall, forbidding library. It looked the scene of a murder mystery. Massie shuddered. Was the Rivera house always this lonely?

Massie struggled to pull her suitcase up the grand staircase. She was almost at the top landing when Alicia's tap-dancing troupe started up again. The noise pounded into the walls and echoed around corners and down hallways. She ducked into the first room she saw and closed the door, but the tapping was still there. She tried the next room, and the one after that. But it was everywhere. Alicia's tapping was *toe*-dally inescapable. And Bean was *toe*-dally inconsolable.

After another ten minutes of covering her and Bean's ears in alternating increments, Massie had had enough. She fired off a "change of plans" text to Alicia and carefully made her way down the stairs—gripping the banister as if her life depended on it. Which—seeing as she'd rather die than come to in a pair of tap shoes and a bow-tie-bedazzled leotard—it did.

"We both know *Kristen* won't be dancing," Massie confirmed as she pulled her suitcase into the Pinewood's elevator. Bean looked up at her with appreciative eyes. "For one thing she doesn't have the room."

Massie let herself in the front door and found a surprised Kristen doing a crossword puzzle in the living room. The apartment smelled like hot dogs and warm rolls.

"Surprise!"

Kristen's light blond eyebrows went from startled, to concerned, to afraid. "What are you doing here?" She quickly glanced around the room as if looking for evidence of something and then threw some hideous windbreaker under the couch.

"Is someone here?" Marsha called from her bedroom.

"Just Massie," Kristen called back, finally looking pleased.

Beckham, sensing another four-legged visitor, crept into the room and hissed. Bean growled.

"What are you doing here?" Kirsten asked. "Did you . . . hear something about me?"

Massie released the grip on her Louis and joined Kristen on the nutmeg-colored couch. The room felt comfortable and lived-in. Strewn chenille blankets, a coffee table stacked with magazines, the warm glow of lamps. It wasn't echo-y and cavernous like Alicia's or wired like Dylan's. Of course she much preferred the clean lines and bright decor of the Block estate. But . . .

She took a deep breath, preparing to tell Kristen what the others already knew. Her palms felt moist, like she had used too much L'Occitane shea butter hand cream.

"Last night, I kind of knew something that I didn't bring up."

Kristen's eyes grew wide with terror. "Claire told you, didn't she?"

"No," Massie said, not bothering to ask why in Gawd's name she would ever think *that*. "Claire didn't tell me, my parents did."

"How did they find out?"

"That we're moving to England?" she blurted.

"Oh," Kristen sighed, relieved. And then, "Wait, *what*? You're moving to *England*?"

"Yeah, my dad got a job there." Sadness washed over Massie all over again. Saying the words aloud was supposed to help them sink in. But it wasn't working. The news clung to the surface of her skin like lavender oil after a bath.

"You can't just leave. What about school? What about us?"

Bean and Beckham were still growl-hissing. But the girls were too caught up in their own drama to interfere.

"I was hoping that maybe I could stay here, at least until the end of the spring semester. And then maybe by then—"

"Mom," Kristen called before Massie could even finish. "Can Massie stay with us for a while?"

"As long as it's okay with her parents," Marsha called back.

Massie had yet to run this idea with William and Kendra, but how could they possibly object? It was a win-win for all of them. "They're fine with it," she called back.

"Done." Kristen smiled, quickly folding the ruby red blanket by her feet and draping it over the back of the couch. "I mean, we'd have to share my room and the animals might have a hard time at first, but we'll figure it out."

"We can host the Friday night sleepovers here!" Massie announced, trying to imagine five girls jammed into a closet-sized bedroom. "Or in the limo," she joked.

Kristen bit her lip. "Maybe you could have them at Alicia's or something."

"I was just kidding about the—"

"No, it's not that."

Massie narrowed her eyes.

"I won't really be able to stay up that late on the weekends for a while."

"Why? Are you sick or something?"

"No." Kristen began stacking and restacking the magazines. "I've been meaning to tell you . . . I got this real cool opportunity." She walked two coffee cups into the kitchen. "I'm an All-Star Soccer Sister," she called.

"Like where you mentor underprivileged soccer players?" Massie wondered aloud.

Kristen padded back to the couch and pulled out the crinkly windbreaker. "Soccer Sisters. It's a competitive traveling soccer squad. I got accepted last week. And . . ." She hesitated. "Well, it means that my weekends—and my life—are pretty much all about soccer now."

"But what about the Pretty Committee?" Massie asked. Claire had her new house, Dylan had her TV show, Alicia had tap, and Kristen had soccer. A loneliness flower bloomed inside Massie's stomach.

"You guys are still my best friends," Kristen said, meaning it. "I promise that will never change." She held up her pinkie. Massie hooked hers around Kristen's. They shook on it.

"Hi, Massie," Kristen's mother said, walking into the kitchen in a robe, her wet hair twisted in a faded pink towel. "I was just going to make some hot chocolate. Would you girls like some?"

"Is it sugar-free?" Kristen asked, for Massie's sake.

"No," Marsha said, confused. "Why would—"

"That's okay," Massie said, knowing she'd have to ease up on some of her rules if she was going to be someone's guest. *When in Pinewood . . .* "I'd love some."

"Same," Kristen said.

Massie found herself grinning and Kristen unfolded the blanket and laid it over their legs. Kristen's mother served them sugary powdered hot chocolate with mini marshmallows in a chipped mug. It was the best hot chocolate Massie had ever tasted.

After a cozy night of TV, Massie and Bean snuggled under

the mismatched blankets on Kristen's daybed. Kristen flipped off the lights and soon the room was filled with a symphony of breathing—snotty purrs from Beckham, guttural groans from Bean, and raspy snores from Kristen. Moonlight cut across Kristen's window, casting a white beam across Massie's face. She covered her head in a rose-scented pillow and tried to drown it all out.

Reee reee reee reee reee!

What felt like minutes later, Massie shot up. Her eyes felt like they had been loofahed. "What is that?"

"Sorry!" Kristen whispered. "It's just my alarm. Go back to sleep."

"What's going on?" Massie wondered, freeing herself from a straitjacket of wool blankets. "It's still dark out. Where are you going?"

"Ssshhh, go back to sleep," Kristen said.

"*Back* to sleep? I don't think I even had a chance to *go* to sleep in the first place!"

Kristen ignored her, pulling on sneakers and double-knotting their laces. Massie searched the room for a clock and found it on Kristen's dresser, where it glowed "4:47 A.M."

She gasp-gaped. "What are you doing up at 4:47 A.M.?"

"Training," Kristen said, acting surprised that anyone would ask. She jumped to her feet and tied her hair up into a high ponytail.

Massie was so shocked and sleep-deprived that she couldn't speak for a moment.

"How often does this 'training' happen?" she croaked.

"Every morning!" Kristen chirped. "Well, except for Fridays. That's my day off."

Kristen zipped up her windbreaker and grabbed an old iPod Dylan had passed down to her.

"Ready?" Marsha poked her head in the room. She was dressed in sweats and ready to jog.

What was wrong with these people?

"Just feed Beckham whenever you feed Bean," Kristen said, and then she squealed. "How fun is this?"

"So fun," Massie managed as she curled into a fetal position and moaned.

Next thing she knew a damp nail file was rubbing up against her earlobe. "What the—" Massie whipped around and bashed into Beckham's cold nose. He meowed and then began pawing her highlights. "Stop!" But he didn't. He kept pawing and meowing. "I'm not feeding you now. It's too early."

Bean shimmied out from under the covers and swatted Beckham. Beckham swatted back. Minutes later, the daybed was covered in fur, $300 highlights, and a note that said: *Change of plans. Had to go.*

"This Louis is a looseeer!" Massie declared as she emptied her luggage into her walk-in closet and unceremoniously dumped its contents on the plush carpet. She couldn't believe how much bad luck it had brought her the past few days. Just looking at the Diane von Furstenberg silk pajamas she'd tried to sleep in at Kristen's house, the baggy boyfriend Diesel jeans she'd worn as she ran through Alicia's abandoned hallways, and the pumps she'd been filmed in at Dylan's made her so sick to her stomach that she couldn't even sip the steaming hazelnut latte she'd had her temporary driver pick up for her.

She sighed loudly and then looked forlornly at Bean, who had curled up in the zippered pouch inside Louis. She blinked at Massie and then cocked her head to the side.

"You're right, Bean," Massie concurred, nodding seriously. "It's not Louis Vuitton's fault that my Goldilocks mission failed."

The realization didn't stop Massie from feeling like she'd just eaten bad sushi. After arriving back at the Block estate before the sun had even been able to melt the icicles off the trees, she'd finally fallen into a deep sleep, where she dreamed of never-ending hallways lined with cameras and tap shoes. When Bean licked her cheek and woke her up sometime midafternoon, she'd been so disoriented she couldn't figure out whose bed she was in—Claire's in the guesthouse? Kristen's in her tiny bedroom? Hers, in her new castle in England?

Massie shut her closet door and tried to apple-X the memories of the past few days. She crossed her bedroom to peer out the windows. When she saw what was going on in the guesthouse, her stomach heaved and swirled again.

"This is *nawt* happening!" She tapped frantically on the window, hoping her nails on the glass would be loud enough to attract the attention of the people going in and out of the guesthouse. But it was futile. She was too far away, and her nails were too weak to make more than a whimper. "That's what I get for stopping my weekly nail strengthening treatments!" she hissed, frowning at her cuticles. Then she grabbed Bean and raced downstairs and out the back door, dumping her hazelnut latte in the melting snow on her way. It left a slushy, poo-colored stain in the pristine white lawn.

"Kuh-laire!" she called as she ran inside. She dodged a stack of boxes and a tall, broad man carrying an empty moving dolly, who quickly left the room when he noticed the expression on Massie's face. Then she stopped. Hard.

The guesthouse was empty.

Massie felt fear climb up her body like it was Jack and she was the beanstalk. Even Bean shuddered in her arms at the sight of it. She'd completely forgotten. The Lyonses weren't supposed to be moving until the weekend, and it was Thursday—moving day.

With the exception of a few rows of boxes lined up by the

door, the guesthouse looked exactly like it had two years ago, before the Lyonses had moved in. All of their personal touches were packed up—the homemade quilt Claire liked to curl up in when she and Massie watched old movies on the couch; the pile of board games the Lyonses used for family game nights; the collection of winter coats and hats and boots that Todd liked to leave by the front door. What was left was picture-perfect Ethan Allen décor. It almost looked like no one had ever lived there.

Massie gulped. She remembered the day her parents had told her that William's college friend and his family would be staying with them for a while. She had hated the idea of being forced to be nice to Claire, with her Flori-*dull* wardrobe and earnestness. Looking around, Massie remembered all of the mean things she'd said to Claire when she first arrived in her overalls and Keds.

Another loneliness flower bloomed, this one in her heart. Why was everything so hard all of a sudden? Was it payback for leading such a charmed life? Should she make an appointment with Hermia and figure out some way to pay it back as a form of retribution? *Then* would her life go back to normal?

"Massie?"

She jumped so high she nearly launched Bean into a basket toss. "Kuh-laire? *Ehma*-move! I thought you had left!"

Claire dragged a large box behind her from the hallway. She had dust bunnies in her hair and grime striped across her gray American Apparel tee. "Not quite yet," she said, wiping her brow. "Mom and Dad and Todd are out back with the movers right now. But everything's ready!"

Massie stared at Bean, pretending to be intensely interested in the design of her Coach doggie collar. She couldn't
let Claire see the panic that had been painted on her face
like the original Picasso her father just sold. She swallowed a
few times, willing her anxiety to disintegrate like a packet of
Splenda in iced tea before she glanced back up.

"What happened to your neck?"

"Beckham," Massie said, covering the scratches MAC
failed to conceal.

Claire had a small smile on her lips, but she looked sad,
too. "Oh."

"Everything's changed so much . . ." Massie leaked. Her
voice trailed off as she looked helplessly around the guesthouse. She shrugged again, her shoulders spelling out *See
what I mean?*

"How were your sleepovers?" Claire asked, falling onto the
couch and resting her Keds on the coffee table the way she
always did when her mother wasn't around to scold her.

"Ugh, don't ask," Massie said, covering her eyes with
her hands and pressing her palms tightly against them. She
breathed in their soapy scent from her Philosophy Amazing
Grace hand wash.

"That bad?" Claire asked, shocked.

"Let's put it this way . . ." Massie said, inspired by memories of watching DVDs on this couch with Claire so many
times. "Dylan's house was *The Real World*. Alicia's estate was
Happy Feet. And Kristen's was *While You Were(n't) Sleeping*
meets *Bend It Like Beckham*, and by 'bend' I mean 'claw my

hair out.'" She pulled her hands away from her eyes and smiled ruefully at Claire.

"I'm sorry," Claire sympathized. She brushed away her bangs and raised her eyebrows. "So what now?"

"Now . . ." Massie smiled hopefully. "Now, can I go with you to your new house?"

Claire hesitated, looking around the empty living room. "It'll be disorganized for a while. Probably worse than Dylan's locker. And you might have to sleep in the new den until all the beds arrive . . ." Claire continued.

Massie nodded her head. "S'okay." She didn't care if she had to sleep in Bean's bed. She'd take it. It was either that or a castle across the pond. And she was running out of options.

STATE OF THE UNION	
IN	**OUT**
Reality check	Reality TV
Tap blues	Tap shoes
Sleeping Beauty	Up
Lyonses' den	The "Blokes'" Castle

"New year, new house!" Claire's father sang as he carried a box into the living room.

Claire sneaked a peek over at Massie, who was helping her unpack a box of her clothes and organize them by color, designer, and season. When their eyes met they both groan-giggled. Jay Lyons had been shouting that catchphrase all day long to anyone who was within earshot—the Lyonses, the movers, Massie, the bagel shop staff, the Starbucks baristas. It had started to weave itself into the fabric of the day like a theme song. And like the newest single from Train, it was inescapable.

When Jay's voice trailed off, Claire paused her unpacking to take a deep breath and marvel at their new house. Even though it was messy and disorganized and had hardly any furniture, the place already felt like home; her bedroom was the perfect extension of GLU headquarters. The sun was angling in through the windows, filling it up with light. The faint scent of fresh paint still hung in the air. The floors shone. And best of all, Todd hadn't had a chance to stink up the bathroom yet.

It was heaven.

Downstairs, Judi was directing the movers as they carried

in the few pieces of furniture that the Lyonses had kept in storage while they lived in the Blocks' guesthouse. Even from inside her new bedroom, Claire could hear her mother exclaiming that she had forgotten how much she loved, just *loved*, that end table or that chest of drawers and how she couldn't wait to see them being used again. Then Jay would add his chorus, Claire would laugh, Todd would get yelled at for breaking something or other, and the whole thing would start all over again.

It was one of the best days of Claire's life.

Once the clothes were hanging in the closet, alphabetized from American Eagle to Zappos, she and Massie turned their attention to the furniture.

"To be hawnest, you don't have a lot to work with when it comes to feng shui–ing your room," Massie said matter-of-factly. She strode over to the single window that faced the backyard and pulled up the white blinds. "You won't get to see the sunrise or the sunset, which can really upset your inner body clock. And—oh, ew!"

"What?" Claire, alarmed, ran to join her at the window. She peered outside and squinted against the bright winter sun.

"There's some old man standing in his kitchen in a bathrobe!" Massie pointed. Then she quickly closed the blinds. "You know what, on second thawt, forget about the view. We'll get those sheer curtains I saw in Anthropologie and then we'll just blow up some photos of the beach in the Hamptons and hang them on the window. Then it'll feel like summer all year long!"

Claire furrowed her brow, trying to imagine her mother's reaction if she hung a poster over the entire window.

"Well, we can talk about that later," Massie said, changing the subject, clearly noticing Claire's expression. "Let's figure out where to put your bed."

"I was thinking here," Claire said, stepping back against the wall and marking the space next to her closet doors.

"Perf! Your bed should always face the door," Massie confirmed, beaming. "That's what the interior designer who remodeled my room the fourth and seventh times told me."

"Great! And what do you think about my desk being right there, below the window?"

Massie nodded slowly, studying the small space. She and Claire sipped the hot white chocolate Massie had just had delivered for the Lyonses. When Claire pulled the cup away from her mouth, she felt a mustache of white foam covering her lips. Massie burst out laughing, her guffaw echoing through the empty room and down the hallway.

"What? What is it?" Claire asked, pretending not to notice her face-foam. She mock-patted her face. "Do I have something in my teeth? Am I out of lip gloss?" She stuck her tongue out at Massie, giggling.

Massie scooped up some of the foam from her own cup and dabbed it onto Claire's chin. "There, that's better. Now you look like just like your new neighbor back there!"

"Gross!" Claire wiped the foam off her face, grinning. She was thrilled to see Massie acting like her old self again. And if it took her wiping 2 percent milk on her face now and then, so be it. She was willing to make the sacrifice. Besides, Massie had once told her that milk cleansers could help clear up the problem spots on her chin.

Just then the chorus from Katy Perry's "Teenage Dream" rang out, interrupting their revelry. "Landon!" Massie squealed, lunging toward her bright pink Rebecca Minkoff tote. She pulled out her iPhone and read the incoming text out loud. "'Wish I was in Westchester to be with you for the big party tonight. Happy New Year!'" She tossed her phone back into her bag and sighed. "You're so lucky that Cam doesn't take the types of vacation that Landon does, Kuh-laire. Being in a relationship with him makes me really appreciate how Brad and Angie stay together. It's hard being so international. I wonder if it's holding me back."

Claire nodded like she understood. But the most "international" Claire and Cam had ever come was when they biked to IHOP for breakfast.

"Yooo-hooo!" Layne's voice floated up the stairs and into Claire's room. Claire side-eyed Massie, expecting her to roll her eyes or suddenly decide she had something more important to do than hang around with Claire. But Massie stayed where she was, blocking out where the rest of Claire's furniture should go and taking notes with her new uMove iPhone app.

"Hi, Layne!" Claire couldn't stop herself from jumping up and down a few times when she saw her other best friend. *How lucky am I?* she wondered, glancing between Layne and

Massie. *One best friend is living with me, and the other lives down the street!*

"Happy move-in day! I brought you a welcome basket!" Layne dumped the basket into the center of the floor and plopped down behind it, pulling out each item one by one. "To begin: a spare key to my house. You can give me yours once you're settled."

"Oh," Massie said, "I'll need one of those, too."

Layne jangled the key on its keychain and then tossed it to Claire, who caught it in surprise.

"And of course, some decorations to mark the occasion," Layne continued, unrolling a roll of purple crepe paper and tossing it across the room. Within seconds, a banner of purple lined the floor. Then she pulled out a big, sparkly, homemade WELCOME TO MY STREET! sign and began taping it to the closet doors.

Massie golf-clapped before Layne got to the next item in her basket. "That was toe-dally nice of you to drop by, Layne. Thanks for coming!" She pushed her toward the door. "We'll have you by once everything is more organized."

"But—"

Massie slammed the door behind her.

"I'll call you later, Layne," Claire shouted, eager to get back to the decorating.

"What kind of budget are we looking at?" Massie asked.

"Um," Claire stalled. Somehow, she didn't think the fifty-dollar Target gift card she'd gotten for Christmas was what Massie had in mind when it came to decorating her—their—new room. She was about to mumble something about how much she liked her old stuff and didn't need anything new when Todd poked his head inside her door.

"What, Todd?" she huffed. He took that as a sign to come in.

"Oh, nothing," he said, mock-casually. Claire narrowed her eyes. Her brother was up to something.

He strolled over to Massie. "So I hear you'll be living with us for a while."

Massie didn't look up as she examined the gold-coated nails she'd had manicured for the Marvils' party. Todd didn't wait for an answer before continuing.

"I just wanted to warn you about how things will work around here in our new house, now that you'll be sharing a bathroom with me."

Claire's heart starting beating in triple time like it did whenever her brother was about to embarrass her. Massie kept her eyes on her hands.

"The thing is, I'm a man—"

Claire snorted.

"—who likes to take his time in the mornings. The showering, the combing of the hair, the shaving and the aftershave . . . it all takes time to look this good." Todd gestured to his Umbro shorts and Yankees tee. Claire snorted again. She could see the hint of a smile curl up on Massie's mouth.

"So if you ever have to really *go*, and I'm in there, just knock on the door, sweetheart," Todd concluded.

"Get out, Todd!" Claire ushered her brother out of the room and then turned back to Massie, an apology for being related to him already forming in her throat. But Massie was chuckling softly.

"Kuh-laire, we are going to have some *fun* with him while I'm here," she said mischievously, her eyes flashing.

Claire grinned, flooded with relief and excitement. She couldn't believe how well Massie was handling all this—her small bedroom, her non-gourmet snacks, her annoying brother. Living with Massie was going to be even more fun than living in her guesthouse!

With Massie in such a good mood, Claire decided it was time to mention her Friday night photography class. But "I'm taking pictures of Cam's band tomorrow. Wanna come?" came out instead.

"Sure," Massie said. "Sounds fun."

Claire felt like she could burst, she was so thrilled with how everything was going. Besides, they'd had enough truth-telling for one week, more than they'd had all year. It was time to step off the serious pedal and floor the fun.

Massie checked her cell phone. "Where *is* everyone? We only have a few hours to get ready for the party!"

Claire brushed her bangs away from her eyes and shrugged. Boxes and clothes were everywhere. Why did she ever agree to host the prep-party? She couldn't even see her floor, let alone her mirror.

"We're here!" Dylan burped. Todd thrust one of the two

LV suitcases he had wheeled up the steps into the chaos. After he dropped off the other one Dylan smacked a five-dollar bill in his hand and Alicia reluctantly kissed his cheek.

Kristen came up behind him carrying a stack of garment bags. "Ah-mazing house, Claire! Massie, Old New Isaac just dropped these off for you downstairs."

"Sorry we're late," Alicia said. She moved out of the way as two movers came in and deposited Claire's new bed as Massie directed them. When they left, she flung herself onto it and stretched her arms. "Practice took for-*ev* today."

Massie snapped her fingers to get everyone's attention. "Bring the bags and follow me."

Huh?

The girls did what they were told without question. They had spent years following Massie. And never once had they been disappointed.

"Where are we going?" Alicia whispered.

"I have no idea, and it's my house," Claire whispered back.

She led them down the hall, and into the furniture-free office. Inside, the hardwood floors had been Swiffered to a shine, vanilla-scented candles flickered along the window ledge, a floor-length mirror was propped up against the wall, an iPod was loaded, and open cases of makeup, hair accessories, and styling tools had been set up in five stations. A couch cushion for each girl was also available in case she needed to sit and do her nails. "Old New Isaac is on his way back with hot chocolate and snacks. Sugary ones."

The girls hugged her like Santa. Claire beamed. So that's what Massie did while Claire had been snapping family move-in pictures.

"Let's focus. Tonight is the party to end all parties. And we have *gawt* to look better than everyone else there. I've taken the liberty of using the money we raised to buy some outfits that will work for us all." She pressed play on the iPod. Rihanna's "Pon De Replay" burst forth from the speakers. Ancient? Yes. Sick of it? Never. The girls began speed-clapping with the beat as Massie dimmed the lights.

"And finally . . ." Massie handed each girl a pink-and-white Intermix garment bag. "One, two, three, unzip!"

Squeals and gasps echoed off the bare walls. Massie turned up the music and the girls paraded around in their outfits. There was plenty of noise but not a single complaint.

"I was inspired by Alicia's sale tent. We all have our own styles, so instead of trying to make us all look the same, I decided to go with what makes us different."

Dylan had a red-hot Herve Leger knee-length dress that would hug her curves like it was made by Porsche. Alicia had a sultry black-and-nude lace minidress, Kristen got silver-and-gold metallic shorts to show off her soccer legs and a sheer blouse, Claire got a blue-gray satin babydoll dress, and

Massie had a white sequin dress that shimmered like it was made of ice.

Apart they looked like individuals, but together they were fabulous.

"Ahhhhh!"

Massie exhaled in relief and spun around the main dance floor, her nude Prada peeptoes carrying her to the center platform. She glowed under the strobe lights as she shimmied to the heavy, fast beats that Samantha Ronson was delivering from the DJ booth. She knew that standing in the middle of the main dance floor meant she was currently the center of attention—not only was everyone on the first floor watching her, but so were the guests on the second- and third-floor balconies. And it felt like home.

One by one, the Pretty Committee joined her, circling around her and getting into the groove like they were channeling Madonna. Alicia's trademark dance moves rocked her mini, while Dylan's red curls bounced around, complementing her red Herve Leger dress and catching the light. Kristen's smooth, high ponytail and winged eyeliner made her look like a sleek, sassy cat in her black shorts. Claire's satin dress twirled happily around her as she grabbed Dylan's hand and sang along.

Her friends looked ah-mazing, Massie knew. But she had to admit she felt extra special in her sequin dress and black diamond jewelry, her brown hair pinned up to give her the look of a Grecian goddess. And in the center of the dance floor, being passed hors d'ouevres from waiters wearing black tuxedoes as the Olsen twins and the cast of *True Blood* mingled next to her, she felt like one, too.

Every year, Merri-Lee's parties got more and more extravagant. This year, the theme was "Haute & Cold Couture," where the concepts of fire, ice, and fashion were reflected everywhere. Out front, an ice-skating pond had been constructed, where professional skaters welcomed guests with triple lutzes and double axels. Out back, a bonfire and rows of tiki torches kept revelers warm as a live band sang oldies, and fireworks lit up the sky at the top of every hour. And inside, catwalks lined the floors as models walked the runways, wearing red-and-silver Herve Leger dresses and tossing confetti into the air. Everywhere Massie looked, there were famous names wearing designer dresses and suits—standing in line for the buffet stations of hot and cold foods, asking the DJ to play a song, and rifling through the swag bags.

"Food break!" Dylan announced, grabbing Massie's hand and pulling the PC to the nearest carving station. She grabbed a tray of sushi and brought it over to the cocktail table Alicia had snagged from Hilary Duff.

"Best. Party. Ever!" Claire said, her mouth full of brown rice.

Massie nodded in agreement, stabbing her eel roll with her chopstick and pointing it toward Dylan. "Tell your mom that this year's theme is toe-dally inspired!"

"Tell her yourself," Dylan shrugged. "Here she comes."

The PC swiveled their heads in unison as Merri-Lee, clad in a long vintage Calvin Klein and more jewels than Massie had ever seen one person wear, sashayed up to them. "Happy New Year's Yves!" She pointed to the limited-edition Yves Saint Laurent handbag that was positioned at the top of a large contraption that towered up to the third floor. "Don't you just love it? We're counting down to the handbag drop instead of the ball drop this year!"

Massie smiled in response and briefly wondered how far out of reach the bag would be if she climbed over the third-floor balcony. Then she dismissed the idea. Her dress was *nawt* made for any physical activity besides shimmying her hips to the music, even though the tote was more tempting than Taylor Lautner.

Merri-Lee air-kissed each of them before wrapping Dylan in a hug while whispering something in her ear. Massie watched as Dylan's face grew pale, even under all the NARS bronzer she'd applied at Claire's. Then Merri-Lee kissed her cheek and floated off to the center stage of the dance floor, leaving traces of YSL Opium in her wake.

Just when Massie was about to ask Dylan what was going on, the strobe lights dimmed and Samantha turned down the sound. A lone spotlight shone down onto Merri-Lee, who was carrying a microphone and waiting for the crowd to grow silent.

"Can I have everyone's attention, please?" Merri-Lee called. Slowly, hordes of people began filing in from the backyard, and Massie had to bob her head around until she found the perfect angle from which to see Dylan's mother. As long as Ellen DeGeneres kept her head still, she'd be set.

"First of all, I just want to say a giant thank-you to everyone for coming out tonight!" A cheer rose and Merri-Lee tried her best to blush, but Massie knew it was just her Shiseido Luminizer. "The new year is a time to reflect on what we see for ourselves in the future—who we want to be, how we can improve, and how anything is possible if we put our minds to it!"

All around her, guests were nodding in agreement. Massie tried not to snicker. Merri-Lee's thoughts were about as deep as the temporary ice-skating rink out front. She looked at Dylan, who was still pale and now looked a little sweaty, like she'd been out near the fire pit for too long. She leaned in close to her.

"What's this all about, Dyl?" she whispered.

Dylan's eyes never left her mother, who was now talking about the importance of family. "She's about to announce the show and reveal the first episode," she said dully.

Massie's stomach heaved and she put down the next sushi roll she had been about to eat and squeezed Dylan's arm.

"With all that said," Merri-Lee continued. "I have an exciting announcement to make! Tonight, for the first time, I'm finally able to tell all of my closest friends the incredible news . . ."

Everyone in the Marvil house leaned forward.

"My daughters and I are the new stars of the next biggest

reality show in television history: *Marvilous Marvils*!" With a flourish, a screen unrolled behind her, lit up with a promotional shot of Merri-Lee, Jaime, Ryan, and Dylan—all wearing matching Marc Jacobs shirtdresses and Sigerson Morrison over-the-knee boots—and the text *Marvilous Marvils: Coming this spring!* spelled out at the bottom. The crowd burst into applause and Merri-Lee curtsied on stage.

"Ehmagawd!" Alicia shouted, barely audible over the noise.

"You're going to be a star!" Kristen squealed.

The PC crowded around Dylan, dropping their rolls and champagne glasses.

"Yep," Dylan said sheepishly, her head hanging down so that her curls brushed against the top of the table.

"This is ah-mazing!" Claire said sincerely.

"You mean . . ." Dylan looked up into the grinning faces of the PC. "You're *nawt* mad at me for keeping it a secret?

"Are you kidding?" Alicia said. "My dad handles the legal contracts for practically *awl* of that network's shows. So I know what kind of confidentiality clause you probably had to sign!"

"We're not mad, we're pumped!" Kristen added. "This is so, so cool."

"Thanks . . ." Dylan said doubtfully. "I just feel really bad that I was keeping this huh-*yuge* secret from you all this time."

"Speaking of secrets . . ." Massie said softly. She looked

at the rest of the PC, one by one. And one by one, their faces grew somber.

"Okay, okay," Alicia huffed after a moment of silence. "Fine. I've been keeping a secret from you all, too."

Dylan gasped. "Are you getting a reduction?"

"What?" Alicia looked down at her C-cups. "Of course *nawt*!"

"Oh," Dylan burped. "Then what is it?"

"I've been . . ." She paused and looked around the circle. When she met Massie's eyes, Massie widened her amber eyes at her, trying to send her strength. "I haven't been reading as much as I said I was. Claire, you can have all the books you lent me back."

"Um, okay?" Claire said.

"I only said I was reading-with-an-r because I didn't want to lead-with-an-l. And when I got an e-reading from Hermia, she told me I'd be the new alpha of the Pretty Committee. But I swear, I don't want to be the leader!"

Dylan burst out laughing. "It's okay, Leesh. Massie's staying with Claire, so you can get back to *heed*ing instead of leading!"

Kristen giggled, then grew serious. "But, um, I have a secret, too. I told Massie already, but I need to tell everyone, because it affects us all."

"Oh, no. Did you lose your scholarship to OCD?" Dylan asked.

"Actually, I got picked to be on a traveling competitive soccer team!" Kristen's eyes shimmered with tears. "It's a *lawt* of hard work. I've already gone to a couple of practices. And while it could open doors for me, it also means that most of my weekends will be booked up with soccer stuff now." She sighed. "And it's safe to say I'll be spending a lot less time with the PC." Her voice wavered.

"We all hate that we have to see less of you," Massie said quickly, not wanting to see anyone else cry. "But what an ah-mazing opportunity for you!"

"Congrats, Kristen!" Dylan said, while Alicia and Claire hugged her. She blew her nose into the monogrammed *Happy New Year's Yves!* napkin.

"Well, now that that's all settled—" Massie started, but Claire held up her hand.

"Wait! I actually have one more thing to tell you all."

Massie froze, startled. She felt like the "Cold Couture" part of the evening. Everyone already knew Claire had moved into a new house. What other secrets was she keeping?

"*RememberhowCamandIexchangedgiftswellhegotmemore-thanthecandy*," she released, all in one breath. The rest of the PC glanced back and forth at each other, silent.

"What else did you get?" Alicia asked after a few moments, tucking her hair behind her ear so her chandelier earrings could be seen.

Claire glanced at Massie, who closed her mouth.

"We're taking a photography class together," she whisper-confessed. "Every Friday night."

Massie lifted her wrist to her nose and inhaled deeply. The

familiar whiff of her Chanel No. 19 cleared her mind and she smiled. It was New Year's Eve, and they were at the best party of the year. Their problems, while not ideal, were not insurmountable. They were like all the homework she had piling up in her locker at OCD—they could wait.

But when Massie glimpsed her parents in the crowd, she realized she still had one very big problem hanging over her head. She hadn't confessed her secret to them yet. And it was time to do it now, before the clock struck midnight and the YSL bag dropped.

"I'll be right back," she called to the PC. "But don't worry—we'll all be fine!"

Massie skipped over the still-crowded dance floor, balancing precariously on her Pradas, until she came face-to-face with her parents. "Mom! Dad! Can we talk for a sec?"

"Happy New Year!" they shouted, embracing her. Kendra's Jil Sander dress felt warm against Massie's skin, and she breathed in the sharp mix of her mother's perfume and her father's cologne.

"How was your day at Claire's new house, sweetie?" William asked.

"Actually, that's what I wanted to talk to you about," Massie said, struggling to make herself heard over the noise of the crowd. "It's nawt just Kuh-laire's new house."

Kendra raised her eyebrows. Massie pinched her upper thigh through her dress. She glanced back and forth between her parents.

"I'm moving in with Kuh-laire," she blurted. "I'm not going to England. I'm going to spend the rest of the year with the Lyonses so I can finish eighth grade at OCD, with my friends."

Kendra and William glanced at each other and then back at Massie. At the sight of their jaws clenched into a tight, sharp line, Massie's throat started closing up.

"Absolutely not," William said forcefully.

"We know this move is hard for you, Massie," Kendra added.

"And we're sorry about that," William agreed. "But under no circumstances—"

"Absolutely none!" Kendra interrupted.

"—will we allow you to stay in Westchester without us. Sorry, but that's the way things have to be," William concluded, thrusting his hands out as if to say, *What can I do?*

Massie felt like the dance floor had become a tidal wave—the ground suddenly seemed to move under her feet, and the bass from the DJ booth drowned out her thoughts. Her stomach swooped like she'd just taken an express ride from the top floor of Barneys down to the perfume-and-makeup basement, and her skin blazed like she was facing down a bonfire that was about to consume her entire life. If she didn't stay in Westchester, she would lose *everything*:

The Pretty Committee.

Her alpha status.

The New Green Café.

The Westchester.

Weekend shopping trips to New York.

Landon . . .

The Pretty Committee!

The Pretty Committee!

The Pretty Committee!

"But . . . it's the Lyonses! Your best friend, Dad!" *And mine*, she wanted to shout. She struggled to keep her voice from shaking. "You've left me to stay with Kuh-laire before. What's the difference between a week and a . . . year? Or four?"

"We're a family," Kendra said, linking her arm with William's and grasping Massie's hand.

"And families stick together," William added.

Massie blinked. This could *nawt* be happening. Of all the problems she'd dealt with this year, it had never even occurred to her that her parents would object to her plans to move into the Lyonses' den.

She glanced behind her at the PC, who were back on the dance floor, waiting for Merri-Lee to get back on the microphone for further announcements. When she turned back to her parents, she started shaking like she was Bean during a thunderstorm.

And then her anger bloomed up inside of her like one of the firecrackers in the backyard. When she spoke, even she was surprised to hear how dark her voice sounded. "You have no idea what you're doing to me, do you?" she said slowly. Kendra's MAC Viva Glam lips formed a small *O* as Massie continued. "You're ruining my life."

Massie's voice cracked. Then she felt a splash of water on her face, and she looked up, wondering if the Marvil mansion had suddenly sprouted a leak.

She felt another one and blinked, wiping it away with her hand. Then she noticed a smudge of color on her fingertip. It was the unmistakable shade of Urban Decay Midnight Cowgirl, which happened to be the exact shade of eye shadow Massie was wearing.

And that's when Massie realized the Marvils' ceiling wasn't dripping. No one was tossing champagne over the railing. The chocolate fountain hadn't sprung a leak.

Massie was crying.

"Massie?" Dylan tried to make out the glitter-embossed girl heading her way. It looked like Massie and it smelled like Massie, but this girl was crying. Sobbing, really. And Massie Block did *nawt* sob. Especially in public.

"*Ehma-what-do-we-do?*" Alicia hissed into Dylan's ear as the girl stumbled into Dylan's arms. Dylan sniffed her hair and coughed up some Chanel. Definitely Massie.

"What is it? What happened?" Dylan asked, more gently this time. The PC huddled around Massie on the edge of the dance floor. She hiccupped.

"I just can't believe this," she whispered. "But they're not letting me move in with Kuh-laire. I'm going to England."

"What?" everyone cried. Massie nodded, looking stunned.

"They told me—" Massie looked around wildly as the lights went out. A hush traveled through the crowd. The PC looked toward the stage where Merri-Lee was holding the mic. She winked in Dylan's direction.

"And . . . action!" Merri-Lee shouted.

And then the pilot episode of *Marvilous Marvils* began to play on the big screen.

Dylan wanted to be there for Massie, but she was riveted to the screen. Either someone in production had editing skills

161

or the camera loved Dylan—but either way, she looked ah-mazing, if she did say so herself.

As the cameras followed Dylan's family around on screen, she gaped at her hair. It made Alicia's hair look like a bad, dull dye job! And her legs? She sneaked a glance at Kristen's muscular gams and grinned. Her legs looked at least as lithe and long. She shook her head in delight as the crowd laughed along with the show. Maybe Merri-Lee had been wrong about the camera adding ten pounds. Maybe it added ten *points* on the hawtness scale. Dylan looked downright spectacular on screen!

When the opening sequence ended, the party guests applauded and cheered. Even Massie had managed to sniff away the rest of her tears and clap her hands. Dylan tossed back another piece of sashimi in excitement. Maybe being the star of a reality show wouldn't be so bad, after all!

She nearly choked, though, when the sound of her burping—the loudest, longest noise she'd ever made—echoed from the screen and landed among the five hundred guests currently captivated by the show's promotional reel. Real-Dylan froze while Reality-Dylan burped again. So did everyone else in the mansion.

From the dance floor, the entire party watched on the big screen as Reality-Dylan burped, tripped, and cried her way through the various scenes she'd shot with her sisters. She got caught sneaking ice cream at midnight. Sleeping with zit cream slathered over her chin. Falling out of her window in her flannel pajamas and spraining her ankle, her lone clog dangling from the branch of a bush.

Real-Dylan tried to hide behind Kristen's high pony-tail, but it was no use. Reality-Dylan was out there for the world to see. And Real-Dylan would never be able to hide her flaws behind her hair or her black AmEx ever again.

Just when she thought it couldn't get any worse, the promo reel zoomed in on a close-up of Reality-Merri-Lee having a heart-to-heart with Reality-Dylan. Real-Dylan felt her hands grow clammy and the sweat begin to pool under her arms. She crossed her fingers in hope that her Dove Clinical Protection would deliver its promise. She wanted to run over to Massie and cover her ears like Merri-Lee used to do whenever she had Kathie Lee Gifford over for dinner when Dylan was a kid. She remembered this scene—she just hadn't realized at the time that it was being filmed.

"Mom, can we talk?" Reality-Dylan asked, the camera closing in on Dylan's fire-red hair and glowing skin.

"I just found out some awful news about Massie," Reality-Dylan said. The crowd in the Marvil mansion watched in silence, transfixed by Dylan's wide, innocent, impeccably accented eyes. "Her family's lost all their money," Reality-Dylan confessed.

On screen, Merri-Lee sighed and began to assure her daughter that the Marvils would never have to worry about that, because she'd set up trusts for each of her girls, which they would all have access to when they turned twenty-five or when they won their first Oscar, whichever came first.

Real-Dylan hung her head, the blood rushing to her face. She was so *ah*-shamed. How stupid could she be? She should have known not to spill any secrets to Merri-Lee once she'd learned they'd be filming a show. And now Massie had to live with the knowledge that the world was going to find out she was once middle-class! She would kick herself, except that her Jimmy Choos were limited-edition, and the last thing anyone needed was another catastrophe.

"Dylan," Massie's voice broke through the roar of the crowd as they responded to the end of the promo reel, applauding and laughing at the wild and crazy antics of the Marvil girls. The lights came back up. People began moving to the outside fire pit to watch the firecrackers or the front yard to watch Merri-Lee film Nancy Kerrigan in a special "Return to the Ice" feature that would air the following week.

"I'm so sorry, Massie," Dylan cried.

"Oh, don't worry about me," Massie said, shrugging. Her tears had cleared up and she looked calm and serene, like Sandra Bullock in her first public appearance after her divorce. "I'll be fine. Everyone knows reality shows are toe-dally fake!"

Dylan sniffled. "They do?"

"They *are*?" Claire asked in surprise.

"Given," Alicia croaked.

"I just can't believe how stupid they made me look," Dylan

said, covering her eyes as a running reel of her flaws flashed before her eyes.

"Stupid? Dylan, did you see that opening scene? You looked ah-mazing times a million!" Massie said.

"You looked like Isla Fisher!" Kristen chirped.

"Scarlett Johansson when she had red hair!" Alicia added.

"Little Orphan Annie!" Claire shouted. Massie gave her a withering look. "I meant, happy and little and red," Claire explained.

Dylan sniffled again. "I mean, I *did* look pretty great, physically speaking," she concurred. "But the burping, and the falling, and the secret-telling . . ."

"Are you kidding me? You'll be the hit of the show!" Massie said, looping her arm through Dylan's. "Did you see how your sisters came across? Opposite of enthralling!"

"Boring times ten," Alicia agreed.

"*Seventeen* magazine isn't going to want to interview a couple of suh-noozers who fight about boys, are they? No, they are *nawt*," Massie answered her own question. "They're going to want to talk to the girl who can burp all the lyrics to Taylor Swift's new song. The girl who can tumble out of a window and still walk away with her bed head held high!"

Dylan felt her lips curl up. Massie and the rest of the PC had a point. *Seventeen* was all about quirky girls like her. Maybe she could even pen her own column! She could get extra credit for English class!

But then she sighed and felt her good mood recede again. Massie was the only person who could manage to talk her out of her bad moods.

Who was going to do it when Massie was gone?

The bass from the band was making Alicia's butt vibrate as she sat on the edge of the balcony, her legs dangling off. She kicked her Manolos back and forth. Next to her, Dylan was performing damage control on Claire's Fiberwig mascara, pulling flecks of black makeup off her cheeks from where her tears were still falling. Massie and Kristen were leaning against the railing, their arms interlocked around each other's necks and their faces more morose than the audience at a Fall Out Boy concert.

When the sky lit up with another round of firecrackers, Alicia straightened up and tried to blot her face with the back of her hand. She realized this was getting a bit ridiculous. The entire Pretty Committee was in shambles. She had never seen Kristen cry so hard—not even during the first, second, and third times they'd all watched *Titanic* together—and she'd never seen Massie cry, ever. Since Massie broke the news about her inevitable move to England, Claire hadn't mentioned Cam once, and Dylan hadn't burped in over an hour. It was like some New Year's Yves version of *Freaky Friday*.

"Okay, everyone," Alicia pulled up her legs and turn-swung herself around until she was facing her friends. The moon shone down on her like a spotlight during the final scene of a

Broadway show. "Tonight has *nawt* gone the way we planned. But the night's *nawt* over yet!"

Everyone nodded in agreement and looked at Alicia with a glimmer of hope in their eyes. Even Massie looked like she was counting on her to come up with some sort of solution to make them all feel better. She scanned through her brain, searching for ideas. She felt like a giant blinking DANGER sign was flashing at her, warning her that she was veering too close into alpha territory, but it didn't matter now. Massie needed her. The PC needed her. She was going to have to face her beta-fears for the sake of her friends.

She pulled her phone out of her Alexander Wang clutch and double-checked the last message she'd received from Hermia. If she had deciphered it correctly, it meant that Hermia was downstairs in the Marvils' library, giving psychic readings again, just like she had on the first New Year's Yves party that had brought the Pretty Committee together. She stood up.

"This is opposite of acceptable!" she cried. "Everyone, get up and follow me." She snapped her fingers twice for good measure, and because she wanted to see how sparkly her OPI Midnight Mambo nail polish could be in the moonlight.

One by one, the PC stood up and formed a line in front of Alicia. She walked down the row, peering at each of their faces. She was on a mission, but first she had to make sure everyone looked presentable. Merri-Lee had standards, after all.

"Massie, you know tragedies are no excuse for unglossed lips."

Massie raised her eyebrows but didn't say a word as she applied another coat of Glossip Girl. Alicia moved on to Kristen.

"Your wing-tipped eyeliner has made a serious crash landing. Have Massie reapply it." She moved down the line to Dylan. "Moroccan hair oil. Plus, the scent will soothe you."

When she finally landed in front of Claire, Alicia sighed. She examined her windblown hair, her pale lips, her skin that looked parched for color. She just shook her head and stepped away to face everyone. Claire shrugged and bit her lip.

"We have to face Hermia and get some answers," Alicia explained. "Ready? Okay!"

Kristen half-raised her hand. "Do you really think Hermia will be able to tell us anything?"

Alicia smirked at the memory of her first meeting with Hermia, but it made her sad, too. She met Massie's gaze and held it. "She predicted we'd all become friends, didn't she?"

Massie gave the briefest of nods while Kristen, Dylan, and Claire all smiled. Then they followed Alicia down the main staircase and down a hallway into the library. The ornate double doors were closed, blocked by a long line of people waiting for their turn with Hermia.

"Excuse me," Alicia called loudly, pulling the PC in front of her. It was a given that she would cut the line to see Hermia (again). This was an emergency, after all.

"Hey!" someone protested. "The end of the line is back here!"

Alicia pulled open the doors and ushered everyone in while two more fortune-seekers yelled at her.

"Can it! This is my house!" Dylan called behind her as she pulled the doors closed.

Alicia blinked when the light from the hallway disappeared. The library had been utterly transformed. Tall candelabras lined the shelves, casting flickering shadows on the walls. Hermia sat alone at a small table in the center of the room, dressed in a flowing purple velvet cape. The table was empty except for a single crystal ball placed directly in front of Hermia. She met Alicia's eyes and smiled, her thin lips cracking against her skin like an eggshell.

Alicia sucked in her breath.

"I've been expecting you girls," Hermia said, breaking the silence. She patted the empty chairs surrounding the table. "Sit, sit. We have much to discuss."

Massie charged forward and took the seat closest to Hermia. Following her lead, Alicia and the others sat down, glancing at each other with wide, shiny eyes.

One of Hermia's long red nails slowly tapped the crystal ball. "There are many closed hearts reaching me now. We must chant to clear our minds and souls of the negative energy before I begin my reading." She clasped Alicia's palm with one hand, reaching for Massie with the other. It was cold and smooth, and a shiver crept down Alicia's spine.

"Oooh—aaah—oooh—dooo," Hermia began. When Alicia

felt Hermia squeeze her hand, she joined in, too, kicking Claire under the table. Claire jumped but then started chanting, and soon, the entire PC was humming along with Hermia.

"It's coming! My vision is coming!" Hermia's eyes snapped open. She pounded the table once with her hand. They stopped chanting.

Hermia let out a long, deep breath. "Your committee has been strong, successful all this time, no?"

They all nodded. Alicia felt her heartbeat quadruple like she'd just done a series of triple pirouettes. Hermia was so *awn*.

"I am seeing things you may not like," Hermia warned, her eyes locked into her crystal ball. She leaned forward, and the rest of the girls followed suit. "Alicia, I see in you a lack of confidence. You must now accept that you have the ability to be a great leader and take charge."

Alicia gulped. Well, at least it was confirmed.

"The blond one from Florida," Hermia continued. "You must carve your own path now. Do not be afraid. You have all the tools you need."

Next to Alicia, Claire choked back a sob. Alicia patted her hand in sympathy.

"The redhead. You will learn that you are worthy of love, no matter what you look like. You will need to learn to accept yourself, with or without Caribbean cleanses." Hermia's eyes were glassy, and she sat unblinking as Dylan's face crumpled.

"The athletic blonde. I see that you're different in many ways from your friends. Embrace those differences. You will learn to be proud of what sets you apart."

Kristen blew her nose loudly.

"Ah, the girl with the power. Massie." Hermia didn't blink as she stared deeper into the crystal ball. "You, my dear, are facing many changes. Changes that don't include anyone named Larry, or Lyle, or L . . . Landon, is it? No, I see changes that include someone named J . . . J . . . aha! James. I see his face now."

"James?" Massie repeated, pulling the crystal ball toward her.

"Patience!" Hermia thundered. Alicia jumped in her seat. Massie reluctantly slid the ball back to Hermia and settled back in her chair.

"As I was saying," Hermia continued. "You are all facing big changes on the horizon. Make no mistake—they will be difficult." She looked sternly at each of them, but then her face softened. "But you have the resources to make the best of them." And then she covered her crystal ball.

Alicia let Hermia's words sink in like her Fresh Mamaku Night Serum. And just like the cream, they went on thick, but dissolved quickly. She side-glanced at the rest of the PC.

"Massie?" Alicia whispered, cutting across the silence of the library. Massie's face was wearing an expression Alicia had never seen before: fear.

"I can't do this," Massie whisper-croaked. She looked

around wildly at the PC. She licked her dry lips. "I can't move to England. I . . . I'm not ready."

"You're Massie Block." Claire ran her fingers through her bangs and sympathy-tilted her head toward Massie. "If anyone can get through this, it's you."

But Massie shook her head, biting her lower lip. Alicia was speechless. She'd never seen Massie intentionally inflict distress upon one of her best features. It was unnerving, and her fingers were flexing for the nearest tube of gloss to toss her way when Massie continued.

"The Pretty Committee means everything to me," she explained, shrugging her shoulders in defeat. "Look at what I made us. We're nawt just the girls who rule OCD, or the girls who lip-kiss the hawtest boys in eighth. We're more than just the crew that gets good grades and wears the best clothes." She looked at each of them, one by one. "We're best friends."

Alicia felt another tear itching behind her eyelid. She could see the others' lips trembling. Even Hermia looked touched, dabbing at the corners of her eyes with the sleeve of her purple cape.

"OCD wouldn't have been half as ah-mazing without you all," Massie continued. Her voice wavered but then grew stronger. "My *life* wouldn't have been half as ah-mazing. You all bring something toe-dally unique to my life, every day. And I cannawt imagine how I'll survive in England without you."

Massie's amber eyes were bright, reflecting the candlelight

that still lit up the library. She stood up, her Pradas scraping the floor as she made her way to Kristen, who swivel-stood to meet her. Alicia was still dumbfounded. The whole thing was like a scene out of *The Wizard of Oz*, right before Dorothy got on the balloon and stopped to tell the Scarecrow, the Tin Man, and the Cowardly Lion her goodbyes. Alicia shuddered at the thought. Massie was *much* better dressed than poor old Dorothy had been.

"Kristen, you're the smartest person I know," Massie said, holding her at arm's length. "I don't think I say it enough—"

"*Ever*," Dylan cough-interrupted.

"—but it's true. You're a big part of why the PC gets the respect we do." She leaned in closer and dropped her voice to a whisper. "And why we get away with what we do."

Kristen cackled, her phlegmy laugh echoing.

"You work harder than anyone I know. Harder than my mom works at staying young, even." Massie took a deep breath and concluded, "You've shown me that anything can be done if you want it badly enough."

Kristen seized Massie and held her in a tight hug, sobbing, for what felt like hours. Alicia slyly checked her Tag Heuer. She was touched, but she didn't want to miss the YSL drop. Finally, Massie pulled away from Kristen and teetered her way to Alicia. She cleared her throat before speaking.

"Never underestimate the role of a beta," Massie began. "Alicia, you never stopped challenging me. I've learned from you how to not just *become* an alpha, but how to *stay* an alpha. And I can-*nawt* thank you enough for that. It's made me a better person."

As she studied her best-friend-slash-biggest-competitor, Alicia felt her defenses crumble. It was no use, pretending she wasn't a BFL (Beta For Life). Massie could move to the moon, and she'd still be the ultimate alpha in Westchester, and the first person Alicia would try to impress.

"Massie," Alicia choke-croaked, her throat closing up from the sobs that had been building for days. "What are we going to do without you?"

Massie shook her head sadly, a fresh river of tears spilling over her cheeks. "Don't you get it, Leesh? You'll all be fine. I'm the one who has to start fresh."

Alicia blinked, stunned. This whole time, she'd been so worried about how she'd fill Massie's Pradas as the new alpha of the PC that she'd forgotten to view the situation from Massie's perspective. Massie would be starting over, alone, in a new country—no PC, no OCD, no Landon. And where did English people shop? Did the country even *have* a Barneys? Alicia sighed and grabbed Massie's hands. It would be the toughest thing she'd ever had to do, but Alicia knew she had to take Hermia's advice and learn to take charge. For Massie's sake, and for her own.

"My turn!" Dylan burped. Alicia squeezed Massie's hands once more and Massie gave a little smile that lit up the flickering library. Alicia knew that they'd just come to the same realization: The more things changed (the move to England,

Alicia taking over as alpha), the more they stayed the same (Dylan's digestive issues).

"You, Dylly," Massie said, curling a lock of Dylan's red hair around her finger and tugging on it. "Hawnestly, you make me laugh more than I ever thought possible. But more important, you remind me with every disgusting thing you do that true beauty lies in our imperfections."

"What do you mean?" Dylan's tone grew serious. She looked behind Massie to find her reflection in the window, and she frowned, examining her body in the candlelight until Massie blocked her view.

"What I mean is, you're perfect the way you are. Which taught me that we *all* are." Massie broke into a grin. "And you've taught me not to take life so seriously. It's only life, after all."

"Aw, shucks," Dylan said, hooking her arm around Massie. Then she pointed to Claire, who was standing outside the PC circle of love, looking down at the ground and shuffling her feet. "Don't forget about her."

"As if I could!" Massie scoffed. She pulled Claire into the group and forced her to look up. "Kuh-laire, I seriously doubt that England will have anyone like you."

Claire sighed. "Unfashionable?"

"Down-to-earth," Massie answered matter-of-factly. "Grounded. Loyal. And not just to me, but to everyone and everything. Even your Keds." She shook her head. "No matter how much I tried to break you of it, you're always exactly . . . you."

"Sometimes I wonder if that's such a good thing," Claire whispered.

"It's everything, Kuh-laire," Massie said fiercely. "I never told you how much your moving to Westchester and into my house changed me. You showed up out of the blue and I *hated* you for making me learn from you. I hated it, because it meant that I wasn't always right. Because it meant that I needed to learn not to judge people based on clothes or bad haircuts or whether they know how to tell real Swarovski crystals from rip-offs!" Massie sniffled and her voice caught again. "Kuh-laire, you turned up in Westchester and proved to me that the truest friends can appear at any time, and from anywhere. Even from a weird city in another state where people shop at strip malls." Her voice dropped to whisper, and her lower lip trembled. "Even when people like me don't deserve them."

At those words, the entire PC lost it. Alicia doubled over, her stomach heaving from the sobs that racked her C-cups. Dylan and Kristen were openly crying, clutching at each other, while Massie and Claire folded themselves into a never-ending hug. Alicia had never realized that all this time, Massie needed the PC just as much as, if not more than, the PC needed her. It had been a two-way street, a give-and-take that benefited everyone. Only now England had come in and thrown a giant pothole into the thick of things, causing a total traffic jam.

After several minutes of tears, a new voice spoke up.

"Massie," Hermia said, rising from the table, her cape

flowing around her. "There is always a lesson if one looks long enough and deep enough to find it. I suspect you've discovered that about yourself?"

Massie nodded, wiping away the remains of her tears, leaving streaks of wet, black mascara raining down her cheekbones.

"You need to remember all the times you've taken a lump of coal and turned it into a diamond," Hermia continued wisely, clasping her fingers in front of her. They were lined with sparkling jewels.

"Like when I moved in to your guesthouse," Claire smiled. "You definitely made the best of that situation."

"And when we got stuck in the BOCD trailers," Dylan blurted. "You turned them into the hawtest place in school!"

"Your first kiss with Derrington." Kristen winked.

"Last summer, when your parents forced you to get a job and you became the top Be Pretty seller of all time," Alicia added.

"And when we all got cuh-rushed by our crushes last year, you enforced a mandatory boyfast and formed the NPC," Dylan recalled.

"There are so many ways you've always made the best out of bad situations," Kristen nodded.

"It's why you were our alpha," Claire said softly. Her words hung in the air. The past tense struck Alicia, and she could tell it affected the others, too.

"A grand adventure awaits you, Massie," Hermia said,

sweeping her caped arms out like she was twirling around the fields of England herself. "I can't wait to see what you make sparkle next!" She winked at Massie and began gliding out of the library. Then she paused on the threshold and looked back at the Pretty Committee.

"And remember," she added mysteriously, winking. "I *will* see it. I always do!"

The tiki torches that decorated the Marvils' backyard flickered just like the candles inside the library, only more luminous. Massie shivered and wrapped her arms around her as the December wind whipped through the trees. When the PC had recovered from Hermia's visions and left the library, Dylan had led them outside to a hidden spot behind the stage, where JLo and Marcc were singing a duet to the rowdy crowd, so they could have some privacy.

It was a little too private, though. They stood around, stomping their feet to avoid frostbite, and avoided each other's eyes in silence. Massie couldn't think of anything else to say. She'd already spilled her guts to the PC, revealing more secrets than a Katie Holmes tell-all. Her throat ached from all the crying, and there wasn't enough Too Faced concealer in the world to hide the raw spots on her cheeks, which were chapped from the combination of tears and cold. Despite being rich again, she felt utterly spent.

When JLo launched into another song, Massie had had enough. She clapped her hands twice—partly to get the blood circulating in them again—and got the PC's attention. They all stood a little straighter, like Alicia's dance teacher was grading them on their posture. It felt like old times.

"It's New Year's Eve, and we're at the biggest, best party of the year," she began. "We need to put what just happened behind us. What happened in the library, stays in the library."

"Like Vegas?" Kristen giggled, but then covered her mouth with her hand. It was too soon for laughing.

"Massie's right," Alicia declared.

Massie nodded, and the PC huddled together for a big group hug, goose-pimpled arm against goose-pimpled arm. They leaned their heads together until their foreheads were touching, forming a pinnacle that Massie knew would withstand any distance they were forced to deal with. It was highly unfortunate that it couldn't withstand the bitter temperatures.

"Here's to the Triple F," Dylan said sadly. "Fab Five Forever."

Everyone's final tears dropped from their faces and landed on the ground in the center of their circle. Massie inhaled the moment and tried to force it into a memory. *Click*. Her mental snapshot worked, so she sniffled one last time before reaching for her Glossip Girl Auld Lang Citrus and applying a thick orange-y coat. It was so frozen it felt like Massie was stabbing her lips with the brush as the little crystals of ice met her mouth.

"Nothing a little gloss can't cure, right?" she said, trying to lighten the atmosphere.

"Massie?"

"Mom?" Massie cocked her head when she heard the sound

of her mother's voice. She peered into the flickering darkness. "Is that you?"

Kendra stepped out of the shadows, her arms wrapped tightly around her camel coat. When she spoke, her breath came out in little puffy clouds. "I'm so sorry to interrupt, girls, but I need to grab my daughter for a moment." She turned her gaze on Massie, raising her eyebrows as if to ask, *Is that okay?*

She squeezed the PC one last time and then pulled away and grudgingly Prada-paraded over to her mother. She couldn't help but still be angry at both her parents for not letting her move into Claire's new house for the rest of eighth grade. She felt another knot form in her stomach. She could still hear Hermia's words playing on repeat in her mind, and she tried to focus on them as she followed Kendra to a cozy spot under a heat lamp. Kendra wrapped her cashmere-mittened hands around Massie's and began rubbing them to warm them up. Massie shivered.

"We talked to Jay and Judi Lyons," Kendra said carefully.

Massie's cheeks started to thaw, and she practiced turning up the corners of her mouth to see if her face was finally unfrozen. It felt okay, so she tried lifting her eyebrows. They wiggled up and down.

"You must have a really good friend in Claire, Massie, because they practically begged us to let you stay." Kendra paused and then sighed, looking resigned to her daughter's fate. "You can finish the year here and live with the Lyonses."

Massie almost screamed in pain when her jaw dropped. Clearly her face wasn't entirely thawed yet. She stared hard at her mother. Had she heard Kendra right? Had the frostbite traveled to her brain?

"What?" she breathed.

"Your father and I were angry that you made all these plans without talking to us first. And we were hurt that you didn't want to be with us," Kendra continued. "But we should have realized . . ." Her voice trailed off and she fixed her big bright eyes on Massie. "We understand that we're uprooting you in your last semester of middle school. And we know how unfair that is."

Massie slumped down into the bench under the heat lamp and tried to clear her mind of the music and lights and sushi and *Marvilous Marvils* promos and Hermia visions that made up the bulk of her night. What was her mother talking about? Why did her parents keep telling her things and then taking them back? Big, huh-*yuge*, life-changing things?

Kendra sat down next to her. "So even though we'll miss you, you can stay." She smoothed a lock of Massie's hair so it fell behind her ear. "Promise me we'll Skype every day?"

Massie just looked at her. Her skin felt prickly and sharp, and the heat coming from the lamp above was too hot, too bright for her to handle. She tried to register what her mother was saying—that she didn't have to go to England yet, that she could stay in Westchester and OCD and spend the rest of the year with the Pretty Committee. And with Landon!

Landon. Massie felt her heart sink deeper into her chest.

What had Hermia said about Landon? That she didn't see him in her vision of Massie? That Massie was destined to have a great adventure, and that she could turn any lump of coal into a sparkling diamond?

Kendra was waiting for a response, looking expectantly at Massie as she sat there, vacillating wildly between feeling too hot and too cold, like fire and ice, just like the theme of the party. She stared helplessly at her mother. An hour ago, hearing those words would have made her night.

But after talking with Hermia, Massie couldn't help but wonder if the universe was offering her the perfect gift, and it wasn't a black diamond bracelet or a Louis Vuitton iPad case. It was the gift of the unknown. Of adventure. Of new lessons, new places, new people.

And maybe it was exactly what Massie needed.

Claire felt a twinge of guilt run through her bloodstream as she watched the next band set up their instruments and perform a quick sound check. The lead singer was a woman with wild purple hair and a tight red dress, but somehow, she reminded Claire of Cam, all proud and confident as she strummed her guitar and said "Testing, testing" into the microphone. Cam and the band were playing their first gig at a small house party on the outskirts of Westchester. Claire tried to picture the scene as she followed Alicia, Dylan, and Kristen to the edge of the dance floor where the crowd was thicker, the temperature was warmer, and tuxedoed servers held out trays of food and drink.

As she watched another set of fireworks blast off over the trees, she doubted Cam's party was anything like this one. Instead, it was probably low-key and quiet, cozy and simple—the kind of party she was used to. She pulled out her phone from the shiny clutch purse she'd borrowed from Dylan and began thumbing him a text message. She'd been so preoccupied by the Massie situation that she'd forgotten to check in with him all night, and she was aching to hear from him.

Claire: Hey Music Man! How's it going at ur 1st gig?

Cam: You caught me just between sets! We're a hit

Claire: I knew u would be! <3

Cam: How's the Marvil party?

Claire paused, her thumbs frozen over her keypad. How could she explain to Cam how utterly exhausting and yet equally exhilarating this party had been so far? It was almost too much. But Cam was her boyfriend, and he'd always said the right thing at the right time.

Claire: It's complicated. Massie's not staying at my house this year :(

Cam: England's back on?

Claire: According to her parents, it was never off.

Cam: U will still have me around. I'm gr8 at insults ;)

Claire tried to smile at Cam's last text, but his words struck her. Is that what everyone thought—that Massie just threw around insults as often as she threw around money? She licked her chapped lips and glanced around for Massie, who was still huddled under a heat lamp a few feet away. Massie and Kendra were talking intently, their matching amber eyes flashing like the twinkle lights that were still strung up over the Marvils' roof. Maybe when Claire had first moved into the Block guesthouse, it had felt like Massie insulted her at every turn, just for the sake of it. But getting to know Massie, and witnessing tonight's big reveal of truth, made her realize something: Massie wasn't always trying to insult her. It wasn't a game, or something she did just for gossip points. It was Massie's way of trying to help Claire.

And maybe it could be misinterpreted as meanness, but that was just Massie. She was who she was. Just like Claire couldn't change into what Massie had first wanted her to be, Massie couldn't change, either. And Claire didn't want her to. She wanted Massie, the true Massie, the one who taught Claire the difference between silk and synthetic, to always be her friend.

And now her best friend was moving away, and there was nothing they could do about it. Like Layne Abeley's wardrobe, it was a fact they were all going to have to live with.

She tucked her bangs behind her ear and sighed, surveying the party. It looked like everyone else was having a blast. Now that the house band was back onstage, the lead singer shimmying in her red dress and crooning into the microphone, the dance floor was packed again as the crowd sang along and waved their hands in the frigid air. Behind her, clusters of friends were scooping up caviar and cream puffs. Two videographers were broadcasting a live feed of the party onto the back of the house, and a professional photographer was snapping candid shots of people in front of the roaring fire pit. Claire watched as two blond girls approached the photographer for their turn.

"Say cheese!" the photographer called. The taller blonde nudged the shorter one and they giggled when the flash went off.

Claire's smile faded. With Massie moving, would she ever

again be able to take a picture with her best friend like that?

A fresh batch of hot tears pooled behind her eyelids and she blinked rapidly to clear them. She couldn't cry again. But she was worried times ten about what was going to happen to her when Massie left. She wiggled her toes and looked forlornly at her Rock & Republic platforms. Who was going to be hawnest about Claire's Keds? Who was going to make an emergency call to Jakob when her bangs were too shaggy? She glanced at her phone, still resting in the palm of her hand. Who was going to listen to her when she fought with Cam?

It was all too unfair. She cleared her throat and inched closer to Alicia, Dylan, and Kristen. The band finished a song, the crowd cheered and chatted, and then it was quiet for a moment. The remaining members of the PC looked at each other.

"And then there were four," Dylan mumbled. Her words rang ominous in Claire's ears.

"We'll get through this, right?" Kristen asked, her eyes shifting from one girl to the next.

For a long minute, no one answered. Claire kept opening her mouth, but no words were coming out. Alicia was looking at the ground so intently that Claire wondered if the answers to their questions about the future of the Pretty Committee were etched in the grass. And Dylan was burping her misery into the freezing cold night air.

Kristen's question spun around and around in Claire's mind until she grew dizzy at the thought of it. She remembered the last time the PC had fractured, when Alicia had created the SoulM8s with the PC's crushes and Massie had formed the MAC with a group of models from Manhattan. That time, Claire had been forced to choose between the two cliques, and it had nearly ruined her.

Claire finally found her voice. "I don't think we have another option. We *have* to get through this."

Kristen looked relieved, and Dylan and Alicia smiled at her. Claire glanced over at Massie and Kendra. They were still in deep conversation, looking more serious than Lindsay Lohan's legal problems. Claire frowned. What on earth could they be talking about? Didn't Kendra know that Massie needed to spend all her remaining free time in Westchester with the PC?

She was so focused on watching Massie and Kendra that she didn't see her own mother dodging her way through the dance floor until she landed in front of her.

"Claire-bear!" Judi beamed, hugging her daughter. Claire returned the hug, wrapping her arms around her mother and inhaling her familiar scent. There were moments in a girl's life when she needed her mother more than anything, and this was definitely one of those times. She was about to start sobbing into her mother's shoulder when Judi pulled back and grinned widely at Claire. "Did Massie tell you yet, hon? We talked to the Blocks, and your father and I convinced them to let Massie stay. She can move into your room!"

Claire gaped as Judi mother-smothered her in another hug. The Blocks had caved? Massie wasn't moving to England? A tidal wave of relief washed over Claire. Massie was staying! The PC didn't need to elect a new Ralpha

(Replacement Alpha)! They'd be able to graduate from eighth grade together, start high school together, learn how to drive together, go through finals together, cheer Kristen on at soccer games together, watch Alicia perform at dance competitions together, attend the red-carpet premiere of *Marvilous Marvils* together . . . Claire was growing giddier by the minute. She never thought she'd be excited for the stress and pressure that high school would bring, but now that she knew she and Massie would be tackling it all together, she couldn't wait.

Judi disappeared into the crowd and Claire tried to contain her excitement, but it was like Perez Hilton trying to contain the juiciest gossip: impossible times ten. She was about to spill the ah-mazing news to the rest of the PC when she side-eyed Massie, who was finally getting up from her intense conversation with Kendra and heading back over to the PC. She felt a thousand butterflies flap their wings inside her stomach, but then she remembered: It was Massie's good news to break, not hers. And she was going to let Massie deliver it like she was Katie Couric on the nightly news.

Claire discreetly squealed when she saw Massie finally head her way. She was glide-striding confidently over to them, her Rachel Roy dress glittering like the stars, when the light hit Massie's face and Claire could see it clearly. She stopped squealing immediately. The butterflies in her stomach dropped to the ground like someone had just released a bug bomb inside of her.

For someone who was about to announce the best news the PC could ever hear, Massie sure didn't look thrilled about it. In fact, Claire realized as she came closer, Massie looked ready to deliver the worst news of Claire's life.

Claire made a desperate beeline for the nearest candy station. Luckily it was just next to the hot chocolate and coffee bar, so she filled her hands with various gummies and dashed back to the PC just as Massie arrived, still looking glum. Claire popped all the candy in her mouth. She wasn't sure what was about to happen, but it felt like a sugar emergency.

"Everything okay, Massie?" Dylan asked.

Claire, still chewing her loot, leaned in closer. She studied her expression, looking for any sign of relief or excitement—anything that would match what Claire's mom had just told her. But instead, Massie looked like she'd just watched an episode of *Rock of Love*: confused, torn, and a little sick. Then she straightened up, adjusted her white sequin dress, and applied another coat of lip gloss.

"My mom was just apologizing for nawt letting me stay at Claire's," Massie said assuredly. "And she reminded me that Hermia was right. The Pretty Committee's had an ah-mazing run." She met each of their eyes, one by one. "But now we're all off on different adventures. Claire, you have a new house and photography class with Cam. Kristen, you're going to be a star Soccer Sister. Dylan, you're going to be dodging paparazzi. Alicia, your troupe is going to dominate tap . . ."

Her sequined dress caught the light from a torch and reflected small teardrop-shaped lights across Claire's face. "And I'm moving."

Everyone leaned in to Massie for another hug, but Claire stomped her foot. What was Massie talking about?

It took her a few more moments to completely swallow her candy, but as she expected, the sugar gave her an instantaneous rush. She felt more energized—and confused—than she had all night.

"But Massie!" she question-cried. Everyone spun around to look at her. "You're allowed to stay!"

Claire could barely breathe while she waited for Massie to say something. Kristen, Alicia, and Dylan glanced worriedly at each other as Massie's face flushed, then paled, and then finally crumpled.

"I am," she finally confessed.

Everyone sucked in their breath, and the rest of the party fell away. It felt like it was just her and Massie and the PC, hanging out at GLU headquarters, tallying gossip points, playing What Would You Rather, making packing lists, dressing the Massiequin, busting on Alicia's boobs, Dylan's burps, Claire's bangs, and Kristen's boy shorts. Eating snacks, rating each other, and evaluating their crushes. Claire crossed her fingers. Maybe if she wished for it hard enough, instead of the clock ticking midnight and the YSL dropping, she could rewind time and stay with her best friends in the eighth grade at OCD forever. Because that's what would happen if this was a dream. And sometimes dreams came true.

Her friends were proof of that.

"So stay!" Claire urged. The words tumbled out faster than Shawn Johnson's floor routine. But she had to know why Massie, after everything, was choosing to move to England instead of staying in Westchester with Claire.

Massie looked at Claire head-on. Her amber eyes crackled with confidence. Before she said anything it was obvious her decision had been made and would not be undone. "After everything Hermia said, and all of these changes, it feels like the right thing to do. How VH1 would it be if I was still clinging to the past while everyone else moved on?"

Kristen, Alicia, and Dylan nodded, but Claire shook her head.

"What are we going to do without you?" She sighed.

"You don't need to worry about me nawt being around, Kuh-laire," Massie said. Her eyes lit up. "I'm taking the PC international! We have Skype, Twitter, Facebook, e-mail, and who knows what new thing will be out next year? We can talk every day! Summers in Europe anyone?" Massie grinned triumphantly. Dylan and Kristen high-fived her and each other. "I've done all I can do in Westchester. I can't hold myself back anymore. And neither can any of you!"

"Point," Alicia nodded.

Slowly, Claire began to understand what Massie was saying. Just because she wouldn't physically be there with them didn't mean she wouldn't be there at all. She was already so much a part of them, and them of her.

Massie took off her charm bracelet and held it out to Alicia. "You can do this."

Alicia sniffed back a tear and nodded. Massie clipped the bracelet around her tanned wrist and stood back to admire it. "Perfect," she said, admiring the charms she had collected over the years. "Make sure you add more."

Alicia began to sob. "Okay."

They all looped arms until they were a closed circle standing tall under the stars. Love and perfume emanated from their pores and drifted to the sky, forming an invisible heart-shaped cloud that would follow each one of the girls for the rest of her life. No matter where they were, who they were with, or what they were doing, all they'd have to do was look up, and there it would be.

Just then, the crowd began counting down to the New Year and the Pretty Committee joined in.

"Ten . . . nine . . . eight . . ."

Their eyes were full of tears, as they shouted.

"Seven . . . six . . . five . . ."

It was the end of an era.

"Four . . . three . . ."

And the beginning of a new one.

"Two . . ."

The YSL bag touched down.

"One! Happy New Year!" they yelled, their voices getting lost in the merriment around them. Fireworks lit up the sky. The band started up again with a rock version of "Auld Lang Syne," and the crowd, led by Merri-Lee on the stage, sang along.

Claire met Massie's eyes over the chaos and winked at her. Massie winked back, her eyes sparkling, and mouthed, "Heart you, Kuh-laire."

"Heart you, Mass," Claire wanted to say but a swell of emotions left her mute. She lifted her head to reverse the tears just as a heart-shaped firework exploded in the navy sky.

The Pretty Committee followed her gaze and watched as it faded to smoke and then vanished. Leaving behind five tear-soaked faces and another perfect memory.

EPILOGUE

"One Glacéau Vitamin Water and one bowl of Evian water, puh-lease," Massie said as the flight attendant reclaimed her cooling hot towel with a pinch of his silver tongs.

Rule number one of flying was to stay hydrated. Rule number two was to stay entertained, which is why she'd brought the latest *Seventeen*, *Vogue*, *People*, and *In Style* magazines with her, as well as her MacBook, the season-two DVDs of *Vampire Diaries*, a cashmere BRAND throw, and some lavender-scented neck pillows for her and Bean. She spread all of them out on the empty seat next to her and then leaned back, letting the first-class leather seat hold her like a hug.

"Cabin crew, prepare for takeoff." The pilot's Robert Pattinson accent danced throughout the aircraft. Massie felt her stomach squeeze itself and then flutter back to its normal position. Was it possible she was nervous? She'd been flying since she was three months old! Then again, she reminded herself, this *was* the first time she was leaving New York without a return ticket in her Gucci wallet.

William and Kendra were seated in front of her, reclined and sipping champagne, leaving Massie and Bean to stretch out in a row of their own. Now that she was on the plane, her

Louis carry-on safely stowed above her seat, she could finally start to process everything that had happened since the New Year's Yves party:

The Block estate had been packed up and put on the market, its contents shipped to the Blocks' new English castle.

Massie had officially withdrawn from OCD and registered at KISS (Knightsbridge Isle Secondary School).

Massie had purchased—and devoured—biographies and articles on B-Alphas like Princess Diana, Queen Elizabeth, Kate Moss, Stella McCartney, Victoria Beckham, and Sienna Miller, deciding that Madonna and Gwenyth hadn't lived there long enough to qualify as British Alphas.

Instead, she YouTubed recent interviews with the expats to study how they'd managed to tweak their American accents to sound more British. And then decided never to do that.

She and Landon had a heart-to-heart about whether it was realistic to sustain a transnational relationship. There had been tears, but once he had stopped crying, they parted amicably.

Bean had said goodbye to Bark Obama one last time. As she'd watched them run around the doggie playpen in Bark Jacobs, Massie had realized that, just like her and Landon, Bean and Bark would always be friends.

Most important, Massie had said her *goodbye-for-now*s to Claire, Alicia, Dylan, and Kristen. And her parents had promised Massie could come back to Westchester in the summer and stay with the Lyonses, unless they all wanted to come to the castle. Either way they were committed for summer and bound by one of Len Rivera's contracts.

As Massie reached for a magazine, she caught sight of her wrists and smiled. Normally she would *ew*-schew the braided, colorful pieces of fabric that adorned them, but she'd made an exception for the Pretty Committee. Seeing as she was leaving before OCD was back in session, Layne organized a friendship bracelet drive for Massie as a way of getting the whole school to say good-bye. All of her friends, or rather, the people who had always wanted to be her friends, had left bracelets on the doorstep of the estate. There were eighty-seven in all but she only wore five: the four that truly mattered, and Layne's.

The plane began careening down the runway. Bean trembled—she had a fear of flying—but Massie held her close as they peered out the tiny window. The plane went up, up, up until New York, the only home Massie had ever known, began to look like a miniature toy city, twinkling with lights, blowing her goodbye kisses. She pressed her glossy lips against the oval window and sent one back. "I will heart you forever," she muttered.

She and Bean stared out in silence as the plane soared higher. The city lights of her past disappeared behind them as they leveled off over the dark-as-coal Atlantic. Suddenly they were surrounded in blackness: her future, waiting to be filled. Massie rested her head back on the seat, flicked off the light, and wondered what that black space would look like one year from now.

"Would you fancy my nuts?" asked a boy in a Harry Potter accent.

"*'Scuse me?*" she whip-turned toward the aisle and giggled. (If only the Pretty Committee had heard that one!) A smiling pair of brown eyes were fixed on her. The boy who looked the same age as Landon was holding a silver bag of almonds. Thick black hair waved around his tanned face, making his teeth look brighter than her New Year's dress.

"I noticed you weren't eating your biscuits and I thought maybe we could trade." Dimples cut his cheeks, upgrading him from a 9 to a 9.6. If he presented a driver's license and proof of a trust fund, he might be a perfect 10.

"Done," Massie said, handing her plate across the aisle.

"So you from New York, then?" he asked, biting into the warm chocolate chip cookie. Was it possible for someone to chew with an accent? Or were his lips that compelling all on their own?

"Born and raised," she said, proudly. "You?" she asked, regretting it immediately. "I mean, is that where you were? I mean, ah-bviously you were because you came from there but were you visiting?"

Ehmagawd mayday!

He chuckled. "Yup. First time. I spent the holidays at my cousins'. They live right in the city. What a blast!" he wiped his mouth on a cloth napkin and politely folded it so the chocolate skid faced the tray. Massie imagined Derrington wiping his on a sleeve or even the back of the seat. No, they weren't in American airspace anymore.

"Is that yours?" he asked, pointing at her ah-mazing new Louis Vuitton Keepall 55 carry-on.

"Yeah, I got it as a going-away present to myself," she beamed.

"Wow, you must be easy to please," he chuckled.

"Make fun all you want but I earned the money myself," she bragged, even though it wasn't entirely true. It would have been if she didn't use the sale money to buy clothes for her friends. So it wasn't exactly a lie either.

"Really?" he looked confused. "I got mine for free. Kind of comes with the application."

"Huh?" Massie said, eyeing her bag. Her KISS handbook was poking out the top of the bag. "Oh, you mean that?" she asked, kicking it with the toe of her lace-up riding boots.

He nodded. "Quite a nice place. I go there."

Ehmagawd, this Bawtie (British hawttie) goes to KISS?

"I'll be starting there next week," Massie said, restraining from jumping on the seat like Tom Cruise on *Oprah*.

"Well," he smiled, "I'll have to give you a tour."

"Okay," Massie smiled, nervously.

An awkward silence hung between them until he pointed to her wrist and asked, "What're all those for?"

Massie held up her wrists and examined them again in the gray light. "Oh, these? Just some friendship bracelets." She wiggled her wrists around, hoping he'd notice the Tiffany & Co. cuff or ruby-and-diamond ring she was wearing instead. She felt the sudden, deep need to impress him.

He whistled a low, long whistle. "You must have a lot of friends, then."

If you only knew . . .

"I did in New York," she said. "But I don't know anyone in London."

The boy turned his penny-brown eyes on her and smiled. "You do now." He reached out his hand across the aisle. "Hi. I'm James."

Massie almost laughed out loud. Then she held out her hand and took his palm, shaking it firmly but gently.

"I'm Massie. It's ah-*mazing* to meet you."

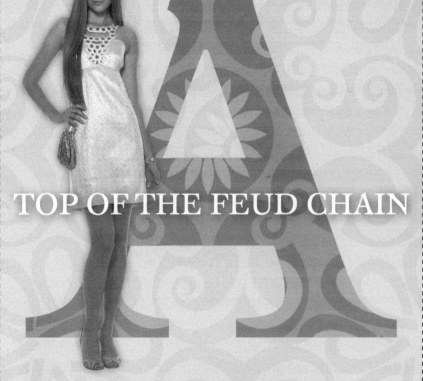

The moment has arrived.
Who is the ultimate ALPHA?

TOP OF THE FEUD CHAIN

Find out in the FINAL
fah-bulous novel of Lisi Harrison's
#1 bestselling ALPHAS series.

May 2011

poppy

www.pickapoppy.com

BOB362

What if a beautiful vintage dress
could take you back in time?

What if the gown you just slipped on
transformed you into a famous movie starlet
aboard a luxurious cruise ship a hundred years ago?

What if her life was filled with secrets, drama,
and decadence?

The Time-Traveling Fashionista is a stylish and adventurous
new series about a girl who adores fashion, proving
that some clothes never go out of style.

COMING APRIL 2011

poppy

BOB361

www.pickapoppy.com

Where stories bloom.

poppy

Visit us online at
www.pickapoppy.com

B0B263